Jonathan woke slowly . . .

And found himself strapped in a wheeled bed. It was being pushed by two orderlies down one of the dim corridors. Unable to move his head, he listened. There were several beds moving in line with his.

They're going to do it to all of us.

The air was sharp with unfamiliar smells. He glimpsed strange figures standing at intervals along the walls. The bed turned into a glaringly bright room. He was aware of a large space filled with people. Their rustle and murmur died down. Someone stroked his forehead, and Jonathan realized his head had been shaved smooth.

Then something cold touched his neck . . .

BROTHER JONATHAN

CRAWFORD KILIAN

ACE SCIENCE FICTION BOOKS
NEW YORK

BROTHER JONATHAN

An Ace Science Fiction Book / published by arrangement with
the author

PRINTING HISTORY
Ace Original / June 1985

ISBN: 0-441-08227-0

Ace Science Fiction Books are published by
The Berkley Publishing Group,
200 Madison Avenue, New York, New York 10016.
PRINTED IN THE UNITED STATES OF AMERICA

For Misha Wittman

ONE

March 28

He hurt.

Cramps made lumps of pain in his legs. His thighs and buttocks went numb, then ached back to life. Itches crawled across his skin. His ribs and wrists and ankles were raw and chafed under the straps that held him down.

He always hurt, but usually they moved him from time to time, before any particular position became unendurable. But today he had been strapped into a wheelchair since just after breakfast. The wheelchair had carried him out of the crèche into a wet, gray Vancouver morning, then into a bus, a jet, and now an ambulance rolling down roads under a harsh white sun. Hours had passed, and he hurt.

The ambulance driver, a bored young man, had polarized the windshield but not the side windows in the rear, where Jonathan sat. The sunlight stung his eyes, making them water. Jonathan thrashed about, trying to escape the glare and find a comfortable position. With a little effort he could have closed his eyes, but he wanted to see what was going on.

The ambulance turned off the road into a wide courtyard surrounded by a whitewashed adobe wall topped with wrought-iron spikes. Palms threw a little shade;

bougainvillea gleamed white and magenta against the wall of a building with a red-tiled roof and few windows.

Sighing, the driver leaned back and spoke to the ambulance.

"Ambulance. Open the rear doors. Extend the ramp. Okay. Wheelchair. Exit through the rear doors, descend the ramp, and stop."

Both machines obeyed. Jonathan's wheelchair stopped and waited. The air was very hot. Jonathan squinted and grimaced in the glare.

"I'll take it from here," a woman said in a voice with an unfamiliar accent. "Wheelchair. Go to manual."

Jonathan twisted himself around, trying to see her, but she had stepped behind him and taken the chair's handles. He tried to tell her it was more fun to let the chair do things; he almost never got to ride in an automated one. But she didn't understand him. Most people didn't, unless they took a lot of time and trouble.

As she pushed him toward a carved wooden doorway, Jonathan saw a plaque in the wall and easily read the first three words on it: *Center for Advanced*. The last word, *Prosthesis,* stumped him. The door opened and they entered the cool, dim interior of the building. Jonathan wished he were back in Vancouver, in the crèche with the other kids. His sun-dazzled eyes took a long time to adjust to the dimness. It was too hot, too cool, too bright, too dark, too strange here.

"Be still," the woman said firmly and clearly. "Everything is fine, Jonathan. That's a good boy." More sharply: "Be still."

He laughed, a choked "Uh-uh-uh." If he could only be still, everything *would* be fine. But her voice calmed him a little.

His head batted against the cushions beside his temples. He glimpsed carpeted corridors and cool, quiet rooms full of old-fashioned furniture, like rich people's houses in TV shows. A door opened: a large bathroom, all green tiles and soft carpeting.

"Here's our boy," said the woman flatly. "A real

charmer." He saw her in a mirror: tall, broad-shoul-
dered, with a round face and short blond hair. She wore
a green shirt and slacks, like the nurses and aides in
Vancouver, but her face was harder and more intelligent
than theirs.

Waiting in the bathroom was another woman, a tall,
slender Chinese with her hair in thick, glossy braids. She
wore green as well, and smiled faintly at Jonathan
without looking into his eyes.

"Hi, sport," she said. "My name is Judy. The person
behind you is Jane. We're nannies. Do you know what a
nanny is? We're sort of like nurses and sort of like
moms. We're here to look after you. And the first thing
we're going to do is give you a nice warm bath."

Good; he was sweaty and itchy, and he needed his
diaper changed. It would be wonderful just to be out of
the wheelchair for a while.

The nannies were strong and gentle, and handled him
with a matter-of-fact intimacy. Still, it was a long time
before he was back in the chair, clean and dry, in new
shorts and a T-shirt. He still hurt.

Most of one wall was a mirror, one of the few that
Jonathan had been allowed to see himself in. He was
surprised to see how big he had become since his last
good look at himself. His legs were long; his shoulders
were broad. His neck was thick and muscular, the result
of holding his head back for years.

His face was changing, too, he saw. A faint brown
fuzz sprouted on his upper lip, much finer than the new
hair around his groin, and his complexion was coarsen-
ing. A few pimples stood out pinkly against his white
skin. His mouth was half open, and his tongue gleamed
wetly on his lower lip. Drool ran down his chin; that
never changed.

The nannies drew the straps back across his legs,
forearms, and chest. Despite them he moved almost
constantly, his hands flexing and extending.

"Is this one's room ready?" Jane asked. He saw
Judy, in the mirror, nod and slide the door open. All
three of them went out into the corridor. Jonathan

heard Jane mutter to Judy, "If Dr. Perkin can do anything for this specimen, I'll be very, very surprised."

Do something? thought Jonathan. As the nannies lifted him from the wheelchair into a crib in a windowless cubicle, he wondered what Dr. Perkin was supposed to be able to do. Teach him to read more? Help him to speak? Jonathan had once seen a TV show about a stockholder with cerebral palsy who spoke through a synthesizer that he operated with his chin. But a stockholder could afford it; a nonstat couldn't. So what would be the point of learning to speak?

Besides, the Intertel Corporation had eighteen million useful members—stockholders and execs, professionals and managers and techs, all the way down to patrons. Why would Intertel care about one of its nonstatus dependents, a useless drooly, veggie spaz named Jonathan Trumbull?

In another wing of the building Phil Haddad sat in his office, designing circuits. He was past thirty, a little old for a computer designer. He wore his hair unfashionably short, showing ears without a single ring or stud. His eyebrows and mustache made three thick horizontals across his squarish face. Assisting him was a turing named Jethro, an artificial-intelligence program who, with three others, inhabited Intertel's central computer.

"Okay," said Phil. On the screen of his plate the circuit glowed red, blue, and green. "Model this one on the last two configurations, Jethro."

"Sure, Phil."

It was a young boy's voice, a clear male soprano. Jethro's face appeared in a corner of the screen; the turing's image was that of a freckle-faced boy with red hair—probably based on the son of Jethro's original programmer. If so, the kid was now in his forties or fifties.

Jethro's blue eyes met Phil's brown ones. "It's not going to work in those configurations, Phil."

"Hell! Why not? Oh, don't say it. Just give me a printout."

The printer on his desk obediently hummed as it flash-printed a six-page report on the circuit's failures. Phil scanned it while Jethro waited and watched and worked on several dozen other assignments for Intertel. Jethro knew that Phil Haddad was more comfortable with words on paper than words on a plate screen. It was a harmless quirk, but it meant his office was piled high with discarded printouts.

"Ah—I see where the problem is." Phil shook his head and tossed the report onto the floor. "Okay, look, Jethro. We're killing ourselves with these super-specialized designs. I need a circuit that'll synapse with *any* neuron, and doesn't interfere with glial cells. Nothing snazzy, you know, just so long as it interacts and doesn't draw any extra energy."

"It has to grow, too, Phil."

"Not grow, just extend."

"If it's got to produce interactive loci all along the dendron, it's growing."

"I won't argue the point. My question is: Can we design such an all-purpose circuit with the data we now have, and will it pose any manufacturing problems?"

"Maybe."

"Quantify, Jethro."

The turing's image frowned. "Sixty-five percent chance of design success. If it can be designed, the cost will be within our budget."

"That's a suspiciously neat figure, that sixty-five percent."

"Aw, come on, Phil. You know I can't do conscious math. I give it to the statistics mill and it gives me a figure. I rounded it off, okay?"

"Okay. Well, maybe it's worth a try. How long will the design take?"

"About six hours, full-time."

"Sheesh!"

"But I can't spend six straight hours on it."

"Obviously. God, it's going to cost a fortune."

"Two to one we make it back in design economies. Anyway, I'll do it in bits and pieces and have it for you by this time tomorrow."

"Good. Give me a shout when it's done, or if you run into trouble. I'll want a critique of the design as well."

"Sure, Phil. Anything else? Bye." The freckled boy waved solemnly and faded out of the screen.

Phil lifted the plate from its bracket on his desk. It was a good plate: hardly thicker than a credit card, with an outsize keyboard under a high-resolution 3-D screen, and the whole thing the size of an old-fashioned magazine. It contained a library of over three hundred thousand volumes, updated once a month; it could access any of twenty private and public infonets; it could interface with most computers; and it was itself a pretty powerful computer.

Holding the plate in his lap, Phil toyed with the idea of getting one of the other turings to work on the circuit problem—Captain Nemo, maybe, or Bonny. But they all conferred inside the computer; competitiveness wasn't part of their programming. Besides, Jethro knew more about circuit design than the other three put together.

Phil shrugged. "Plate, give me the Uncle Scrooge file," he ordered. While he followed the classic adventures of Uncle Scrooge and the terrible Beagle Boys in the century-old comic books, Jethro patiently designed a circuit that would enable a polydendronic computer to interface directly with mammalian brain tissue.

Dr. Duane Perkin's plate sat on a teak desk in a small but luxurious office two floors above Phil's. Perkin's screen showed Jonathan's room as seen from the ceiling lens; Jonathan lay twitching and grimacing in his crib.

"What a mess," Perkin murmured. Jane Fletcher and Judy Wong, standing beside him, agreed.

Perkin rubbed a hand over his prematurely graying crew cut. Sapphires gleamed in his earlobes. In his white shorts and sleeveless blue tunic, he looked more like an aging tennis pro than a neurosurgeon.

"We asked for a spastic," he said, "but he's obviously athetoid."

"I do see some spasticity in his legs," Jane said.

"Just a little. Athetoids have the Babinski reflex, just like spastics." he looked sourly at Jonathan's big toes, which jutted upward and the other toes spread out. "We'll have to do a whole new set of tests. Vancouver made him sound a lot better than this."

"He's not a nuisance, anyway," said Judy. "He doesn't squawk and fuss like Gretchen and Bobo."

"Don't tell me he's retarded."

"No, I don't think so. He tries to vocalize a bit, and he seems interested in his surroundings."

Perkin nodded. "Plate off." Then, to the nannies: "At least he won't go into convulsions every few days. Start the tests tomorrow. But this one's going to be just for practice, if he's usable at all. Vancouver really sold Jethro a bill of goods this time."

After the nannies had left, Perkin looked out the window at the steep brown mountain that loomed over Randsburg and all this region of the high Mojave desert. Almost two hundred years ago this had been a gold-mining town; the mountain had been deeply tunneled for wealth. Now the tunnels were malls and patron pads. The mountain slopes were splashed with the greenery of private gardens and the dazzling white facades of mansions that looked down upon the little city's business and industrial core.

All of it was Intertel property; some of the corp's top execs had homes up there on the mountain. He himself, as a Professional-12, had a respectable status and a comfortable apartment at the foot of the mountain. He had grown up in the corp, had gone to two of Intertel's best universities—Kyoto and Columbia—and was handsomely repaying the corp's investment in him. The Center for Advanced Prosthesis was his idea, designed to his specifications. Its successes had so far carried him six steps up the professional scale; if he succeeded with the current project, he'd become a stockholder—maybe even an exec himself. It wouldn't be an outrageous reward for giving sight to the blind, speech to the mute, strength to the paralyzed, and a vast new industry to Intertel.

He frowned, thinking about the Trumbull child. Well, even a partial success with such a defective would be a powerful argument for more support. Still, he'd have to have a word with Jethro; otherwise the crèches would start fobbing off all their vegges and retards on the Center.

His plate blinked white at him: a high-priority call. "Answer," he said.

The face of Claudio Chang, Chairman of the Board of Intertel, appeared on the 3-D screen. His thick black hair gleamed above a smooth, plump face; diamond ear studs glinted more brilliantly. He looked 30, though Perkin knew the chairman was almost 60.

"Dr. Perkin? I'm sorry to disturb you when you must be very busy."

"Not at all, Chairman, not at all. I'm honored." And surprised. Why should the corp's top exec be calling him like this, without even the courtesy of a precall from a turing?

"I'll take very little of your time. Your project is on schedule, I believe."

"Yes, sir. We have our last human subject here now, and he'll begin testing in the morning. Circuit design is going well."

"Good. Dr. Perkin, I'm authorizing a budget lift of two million dollars to pay for extra turing time and priority matériel procurement. I am afraid we must accelerate the project."

"Afraid? But, sir, that's wonderful news. We'll get right to—"

"Please." Chang held up a plump hand and lowered his eyelids for a moment. "We have a problem. I have been reliably informed today that Flanders Corp is planning a takeover bid against us, sometime around the first of May."

"It can't be true, sir. The Consortium wouldn't allow a corp like Flanders to—"

"The Consortium certainly would, Dr. Perkin. We will of course take all available countermeasures. And your project will be a major one. If our stockholders are persuaded that they stand to profit more from holding out than from selling now, we'll survive. The turings have given us some very attractive forecasts of the market for polydendronic computers, but we must have working models, solid results, before the takeover bid gets serious. Otherwise I'm afraid the stockholders will take the path of least resistance. As they have every right to do."

Perkin tried to swallow with a dry throat. Flanders was notorious for dumping most of its taken-over personnel—selling their contracts on the open market. Many execs and professionals, faced with being sold or taking demotion to patron status, chose the third alternative: seppuku.

"I—I'll do all I can, Chairman. And that goes for all my staff."

Chang studied him impassively for a long time. "I am sure that you will. The welfare of eighteen million human beings is hanging in the balance. Your project could tip that balance. Do not hesitate to demand whatever you need. Your plate is being programmed with my private address; call me whenever you like. And I will call you from time to time." He smiled, a sudden heartening flash of cheer. "Good luck."

The screen went blank. Perkin drew a long breath and folded his hands together on the desktop. Calm. Be calm. Ten minutes meditation would restore the tranquillity he must have now more than ever; he hoped the time would not be squandered.

March 29

Phil Haddad called Jethro right after lunch. "Hi. Any luck?"

The freckled little boy smiled shyly. "Yes, I think so, Phil. Want to see it?"

"If it's no trouble." But sarcasm was wasted on turings, or they were too smart to react to it. Jethro's face retreated to the upper right corner of the plate screen; the rest of the screen displayed a complex, multicolored mosaic.

"Hey, I said simple, remember?"

"It is simple, Phil. As simple as I could make it. The specs are very demanding. This is just the beginning of the circuit. Want me to lead you through it?"

"Just the broad outlines, and then the critique I asked you for. Give me a printout of the details afterward."

"Sure, Phil."

The turing, in his clear soprano, began to describe the components and functions of the circuit. He spoke slowly and without much expression, and much of what he said was obvious to Phil from the image on the plate.

"Can you move along a little faster, Jethro? I can get all this on the printout."

"Sure, Phil." Jethro spoke more rapidly; the images of the circuit components flashed briskly across the screen. Phil began to feel surprise, and then excitement. After half an hour he said, "Uh-*huh*! I see! Oh, Jethro, it's really good. Really elegant."

"Thank you. Shall I go on?"

"No, don't bother. I see the concept, and it's beautiful. I don't follow all the details, but that's okay. Give me a quick critique, and then I'll go tell Perkin we're in business."

An image of the whole polydendronic computer appeared on the screen: a small disk from which eight main dendrons branched and rebranched.

"The new circuit doesn't affect design of the core unit," Jethro said. "It will still have over ninety percent of its original planned programmable capacity, but self-programming capacity will require more room. Each dendron will grow up to eight centimeters overall from the core unit, with sixteen primary ramification nodes

per centimeter. At full ramification each dendron
should be able to synapse with ten million neurons, as
originally planned. I would like to increase that maximum, but it should be sufficient. The core unit, as
originally planned, will control dendron growth and
direction, once the surgeon has determined the implant
site and installed the core unit.

"I see four major advantages in this circuit," the turing went on. "It should not provoke immune reactions.
Having a single synthetic-protein base for all circuits en-
sures that. It won't be susceptible to viral or bacterial attack."

"Hallelujah," Phil muttered. Ordinary organic computers, widely used in agriculture and biotechnology,
easily caught colds, or worse.

"Energy demands are minimal," Jethro continued,
"and we won't have to accelerate metabolism to keep it
running. The chief advantage, however, is that synap-
sing in both directions—from brain tissue to polyden-
drons and back again—will be ten percent faster than
between normal mammalian neurons."

"Very nice. What are the drawbacks?"

"The core unit, in this configuration, responds
poorly to an inductance field, so a small antenna will be
needed. It will be a node on the skin, about the size of a
small mole. The node can also be used as an old-fashioned wire plug-in. It'll be concealed under the subject's
hair."

Phil frowned. "How often will we need to communicate with the core through an inductance field? The
core's supposed to draw on the subject's sensory input."

"During initial testing and debugging we'll need an
inductance field all the time," Jethro answered. "Not
just to instruct the computer—we'll need it to monitor
polydendron growth, brain metabolism, and rate of interface development. As a safety measure, we may want
to dump the subject's sensory input into some other
computer. Otherwise we could lose valuable data if the

subject suffered an accident. But once we have the bugs
out, commercial models probably won't need an inductance node."

"Why not just transmit by radio?" Phil asked, dead-
pan.

"You must be joking, Phil. Signal quality in radio
isn't nearly good enough. You could get rough data that
way, but not the fine detail we need."

"I know; I'm just teasing. What else should we know
about?"

"The subjects may suffer some disorientation until
implant growth is completed—normally, about two
weeks."

"That would be true of any circuit, according to what
you've been telling me over the last month," said Phil
with a shrug. "No other drawbacks? What about cost
of manufacture?"

"Experimental versions will cost seventy-five thousand dollars each, including turing time, assuming a
total of eight to twelve are built."

"Mm." The circuit was three times the cost of most
earlier versions, and five times Phil's annual salary. But
the earlier versions would have required up to twenty
different specialized circuits, so Jethro's design was
dramatically cheaper. "Jethro, it sounds really good. I
want to congratulate you on a brilliant job. Dr. Perkin
will be delighted."

"Thank you. Do you want to get Captain Nemo to
start building a prototype?"

"Not until we get Perkin's approval, but that won't
take long. He'll be raring to go."

Phil leaned back in his chair, stretched luxuriously,
and beamed at the solemn freckle-faced boy on the plate
screen.

"You know, Jethro, I'm so clever I can hardly believe
it. I might even make Professional-4 after this."

"That would be great," said Jethro with a faint
smile.

TWO

March 29

    Jonathan often talked with his secret friends,
the friends only he could see and hear. Once they had
been characters from the TV graphies, who took him
away to their happy countries. As he had grown older,
the secret friends had too, becoming the adventurous
heroes and heroines of the zapper shows.

In the Vancouver crèche a new nurse named Esther
had come when Jonathan was nine or ten. Instead of
parking the kids in front of the big TV screen in the rec
room, Esther had read to them. They would lie in their
beanbag chairs or wheelchairs while Esther read to them
from her plate, holding it up from time to time to show
them an illustration. Somehow the stories were more
solid, more real, than even the most accurate graphies.

Through Esther, Jonathan learned about Hansel and
Gretel, Sleeping Beauty, Alice, Bilbo Baggins, and
Mowgli raised by wolves. He learned of wonderful
places like the secret garden, the Shire, the prairie where
a little house once stood. His secret friends became the
people and animals in those stories; they visited him at
night as he lay writhing in his crib, and told him more
stories of their adventures. They took him back with
them, to explore the mines of Moria and to jog-trot all
night with the wolves beneath the moon of India.

13

Then Esther was gone one day without warning, and the TV screen lit up again. The other kids didn't seem to mind, but Jonathan was wretched for weeks. He entertained himself with his own stories, in which he strode fearlessly into dangerous caves with his bold companions at his side, on a quest to rescue imprisoned children from their jailers in dark and evil castles. Propped up in front of the TV, he looked out instead at unseen lands. Exercised by the nurses, he galloped on a gleaming black charger, a sword singing in his hand as he fought his way through ranks of enemies with the cheers of his secret friends loud in his ears.

Now, on the afternoon of his second day at the Center, he sat in a patio like the secret garden and began to think again of his secret friends. He had spent the morning being poked and prodded and scanned by medics and technicians and machines. It had taken an hour and a half to get down a meal of beef paste, strained vegetables, and mashed bananas. Then Jane had brought him here and gone away.

He enjoyed the glitter of sunlight sparkling on a blue-tiled fountain, the chuckle of its waters, and the buzz of bees in the bougainvillea and bright-orange poppies. Palms and pines cast a scented shade over the brick walks and flowerbeds. He imagined he was in the castle of a great king, awaiting the command that would send him on a quest to seek out and overthrow an evil lord. His reward would be glory and the hand of the princess imprisoned by the evil lord. Now the king had spoken; Jonathan's secret friends gathered around him wishing him luck, giving him worried advice, embracing him. Now, in armor, he swung himself lightly into the saddle of his charger—

"Hey, a new spaz. Hullo, spaz."

The strange voice startled him. He writhed under his straps until he could see the girl limping out of the shadowed colonnade into the bright-green shade of the patio.

She looks like two people at once, thought Jonathan. Or maybe only half a person. The girl was pretty and slender, with a mane of brown-black hair down to her shoulders. The right half of her body was lively and energetic; the left half was thin and stiff. Her left arm dangled; her left leg dragged. The left side of her face was slack, making her smile look wry and sarcastic. She wore a blue T-shirt and white shorts, and looked fourteen or fifteen. A tag on her T-shirt gave her name: Gretchen.

The girl stopped in front of him and stared at the similar tag on his shirt.

"Jon-a-than," she said slowly. "Where you from, Jonathan?" Her accent was clipped and nasal.

He tried to answer, and she spluttered with laughter. He felt his face turn hot and pink.

"Boy, what a superspaz! Not so fast, mate. Talk slow."

Jonathan mumbled again.

"Vancouver? Where's that?"

His eyes widened in shock. She had understood him. Just like that, she had understood him. Hesitantly, not sure she would go on understanding, he said slowly: "Up north. Long way away. I was in the crèche."

"I was in a crèche too." Gretchen lowered herself awkwardly onto the wide tiled rim of the fountain. "In Sydney. That's in Australia, way across the world. They brought me here at Christmas. I hate it here."

"Why?"

"Why? It's bloody boring! Nothing to do. Jane and Judy don't let us do anything, just play with dumb kids' toys. A crummy old wall TV in the playroom, and we only get to watch for an hour before dinner. They could at least let us read, but when I asked for a plate they just laughed. Stupid cows."

He felt a little light-headed at having an actual conversation with a pretty girl. "You can read? A lot?"

"I can read anything, mate. My mum and dad are professionals."

He didn't understand: if her parents had taught her to read, why had she been in a crèche? "I can read, too, a little. Can you teach me to read more?"

She stared at him. "Without a plate?"

"Just draw words in the dirt—anything."

"Why d'you want to read? With those snaky fingers, you couldn't even hold a plate."

He felt his face redden again, more in anger than embarrassment. "I want to know things. Nobody talks to me about anything, nobody. I hear a lot, but not enough. I see words, but I don't know what they mean."

"Well—sure, I'll teach you. Something to do, anyway. . . . Hey, you all right?"

Jonathan was rocking in his wheelchair, grunting and gurgling. "I'm happy."

"Yish! Hate to see you sad, then."

"You're funny. I like you, Gretchen."

She gave him a lopsided smile. "I like you, too, Jonathan."

"How come you're here? Because you walk like that?"

"Too right. I had a stroke when I was a baby. But I can do lots more than I used to. I don't even need a brace or a cane to walk anymore."

"You're lucky."

"Next to you and the other kids, I guess I am."

"Where are they?"

"Getting tested, I guess. We always get tested. That's boring too. Maybe they'll come by later. There's Laury and Bobo and Tran. Laury's fifteen, like me. Bobo's twelve, and Tran's eleven."

"I'm fifteen too. Gretchen, are they going to help us here? Make us better?"

She swayed back, laughing.

"I dunno, but I don't think so. They feed us, and they clean us up, but that's it. I think they like to look at busted brains, just for something to do. Okay, mate, let's teach you some new words."

With a twig casually torn from a bush, Gretchen scratched in the dirt near Jonathan's wheelchair. When she turned to speak to him, she was very close and her breath was sweet. He watched her, fascinated by and en-

vious of the strength and dexterity of her right hand and
the stillness of her left. She was beautiful. Sitting in the
green shade, he thought he had never been so happy in
his life.

The lesson ended too soon, when the nannies brought
the other kids into the patio. Laury was a girl a little
smaller than Gretchen, with short red-brown hair and
freckles. Bobo, whose real name was Bobby, was small
and wiry. He had straight brown hair, cut in bangs
across his forehead, and a sharp little chin. Tran looked
a little like the Chinese kids in the Vancouver crèche,
but with full lips and slightly frizzy black hair.

All of them were spazzes, real spazzes whose limbs
were rigid instead of flopping around like Jonathan's.
But he saw with envy that Tran could walk a little, and
Laury could lean from her wheelchair to pluck a flower
without destroying it. Bobo crawled, pushing with his
left foot and pulling with his clenched left fist. They
could all speak well enough for the nannies to understand.

But the nannies weren't interested in listening to the
kids; instead they sat down on a bench some distance
away and left the kids to themselves.

"What a vegge," said Bobo. His eyes were bright and
cheerfully hostile; his ears stuck out. "Can't even talk."

"Sure he can," said Gretchen. "You gotta listen,
that's all."

"Looks dumb, with all that drool."

"Put a sock in it, Bobo! Smarten up or I'll polish
you." Gretchen limped over and glared at the boy.
"You want me to get Judy and Jane to put you back in
your crib till dinner? Right, then."

"Only teasing," Bobo muttered.

The kids blinked in the sunshine and dappled shade
and bragged about how boring or painful or stupid their
tests had been. Jonathan listened, half to them and half
to the nannies.

"It's more than just a rumor," Judy was saying.
"You know, I wouldn't worry so much if it wasn't that
damned Flanders Corp. I mean, I was born and brought

up in IBM/Sony; when Intertel took us over, everything went fine. But those guys—they bribe the stockholders and then they just gut the corp. Sell off everything, including the people. Remember what they did a couple years ago to Texas Instruments?''

"Yeah," said Jane. "Gee—can you imagine having your contract just—just peddled, like you were a chimp, to the highest bidder? And you have to go along or drop to patron status?"

"A *Flanders* patron," Judy snapped. "No wonder people let 'em sell their contracts. Anything would be better than that. Listen—don't pass it around, and don't tell anyone I told you. I hear if it really comes down to it, we'll go to combat."

"God. Like Zeiss and Michelin? Well, I'm for it— better to go down fighting, let 'em know what we think of 'em. But I won't believe it until Bonny's on the plate with the hard copy.'' Suddenly Jane stood up. "I almost forgot—Jonathan's due for more testing this afternoon. Come on, Jonathan, let's not keep 'em waiting.''

He thrashed angrily against his straps, not wanting to leave the other kids and the sunshine and the mysterious adult talk. Jane grasped the handles of his wheelchair. It wasn't automated; none of them were. Jonathan had figured out that the other kids might be understandable to such a chair, able to order it around.

"Bye, Jonathan," said Gretchen casually. "See you later. We'll watch some TV together."

Jane steered him into a corridor. He was grunting and wriggling, still angry. She slapped the side of his head, a hard, sharp blow that knocked him forward against his chest strap.

"Quit it, this minute. Behave."

He had never been struck before. The feeling was so strange that his movements slowed while he thought about it. It didn't make sense. In Vancouver, nobody had cared about him, but he'd been well looked after. Here they had just a handful of cripples living in near-luxury, but he'd been hit for something he couldn't really control. He considered having a tantrum; it had often worked in the crèche. But here, he decided, it would only get him another sock in the head.

The tests were just a continuation of the ones in the morning: dull, uncomfortable, and pointless. While they dragged on, he thought about the words Gretchen had taught him: the names of all the kids, and some of the plants in the patio. He tried to memorize the letters and numbers on the test equipment so he could have Gretchen tell him what they were. It almost helped him forget the shock of Jane's blow.

The people here *had* to be interested in more than busted brains; they wouldn't fuss this much just to study one vegge after another, no matter what Gretchen said. She was smart, all right, but she didn't know everything. He was as smart as she was; he just didn't know as much. If this Dr. Perkin could do something for them, they could go to a real school, do the things Jonathan had seen people doing on TV: hang gliding, bubble walking, working in spacehabs, playing music.

He dreamed about walking straight up to Jane and clouting her right on the jaw. Then he thought about Gretchen some more. He imagined himself rescuing her from a capsized white-water raft; he entertained her elegantly in his bachelor penthouse; they made love together. She was better than a secret friend, livelier and more surprising.

"Okay, Jonathan, time for dinner."

As Jane slid him from the last of the test tables, he felt a pang of disappointment: he had missed the TV hour with the kids. But Jane seemed more relaxed and friendly now; he did nothing to annoy her.

She took him back to his room, bathed him, put a fresh diaper on him, and fed him. Dinner was a series of purees and pastes, just like lunch. He could eat solid food in small pieces, and Jane should have known it from his file; she must be too impatient, too lazy to take the time. Her body confirmed his suspicions. She fed him with quick, abrupt movements, her eyes on the food tray or on the spoon but never on him. When his jaws clenched on the spoon, she sighed irritably; when the spasm passed and his mouth gaped slackly, she wiped roughly at the drool and puree dribbling down his chin.

"Good for you—all finished. Good boy! That's what I like to see. Now it's bedtime."

She hoisted him from his chair to the crib. Instead of blankets, a kind of tent went over him, made of transparent plastic stretched across flexible ribs. Secured to the crib slats, it kept him warm without touching him.

"Nighty-night, Jonathan. More tests tomorrow. Sleep tight."

"Uh-uh-uh," Jonathan laughed sarcastically. Sleep was the only time he was loose and relaxed; sleeping tight would be impossible. He was angry at everything: the slap, the tests, being fed baby food, not seeing any TV. But he ached with weariness. He slid into sleep and his body calmed. He would wake many times each night, enjoying the stillness that sleep gave him—or awkwardly trying to turn over. He wondered if he would see Gretchen tomorrow.

Perkin always ended the day in his office, checking each of his subjects. Gretchen slept, snoring. Laury slept and dreamed; under her lids her eyes flickered back and forth. Bobo and Tran slept fitfully, whimpering as their stiff bodies grew still more cramped. Jonathan, sleeping, looked almost normal, curled up on his side. With his mouth closed he didn't drool and looked almost intelligent.

Perkin switched to the animal yard. Buck, a four-year-old German shepherd, was awake and pacing his run: ten meters up, ten meters down, over and over without a stumble or bump, though Perkin had removed his sight and hearing centers over a month ago. Across the concrete exercise yard, the chimpanzees Plato and Darwin rocked silently back and forth on their heels. Plato was six, Darwin eight. They were experimental animals only, unlike working chimps, and had lived in narrow, darkened pens almost all their lives. Perkin had created cerebral lesions in both of them, leaving Plato paralyzed on his left side and Darwin on his right.

According to Phil Haddad, the first polydendronic computers based on the new circuit would be ready in less than two weeks, grown and assembled under the care of Captain Nemo. They would be implanted in the dog and the chimps. If the implants took, the kids would be next.

He smiled at his own caution. Of course the implants would take. He hadn't been able to follow all of Phil's presentation on the new circuit, but its capabilities were astonishingly beautiful. Jethro was a smart old turing, and he knew a lot of neurology. Without him, and the three other turings in Intertel's central computer, the project would never have got this far. He had given them the objectives and the broad outlines; the turings had worked out the details, right down to the types of experimental subjects. Not that they couldn't make mistakes. He frowned and switched his plate back to Jonathan Trumbull. Yes, he was mainly athetoid, all right; he slept relaxed, scarcely moving. The scissored legs suggested a moderate degree of spasticity, but nothing like that of the other children. Three spastics, a stroke victim, and an athetoid. Why would the turings have chosen these, out of the fifty thousand brain-damaged nonstat children in the world?

It was, admittedly, more of a technical challenge, and the range of disability was far broader than he had originally considered tackling. To cure spasticity, athetosis, and stroke, all at once, would be a dramatic proof of the polydendronic computer—the kind of proof that Claudio Chang needed to persuade the stockholders not to sell out. Maybe Jethro and the other turings knew what they were doing after all.

Perkin turned off the plate. Almost at once it beeped softly at him: a bulletin. He switched to Infonet I, Intertel's news service. Bonny, the most popular of the corp's turings, appeared on the screen. She was a spectacular blonde, with a sensuous mouth and a high

bosom. Normally she wore her hair in a loose corona
and dressed in bright colors. Today, though, her hair
was drawn back in a severe bun and she wore a sober
gray jacket.

"Good day, members. This is Bonny with an urgent.

"The Board of Directors of Flanders Corp has moved
to acquire a controlling interest in Intertel. The decision, taken at yesterday's board meeting and announced
today, ended weeks of rumor and speculation."

The face of Flanders media rep Nosuke Kuroshima
appeared on the screen.

"Intertel is a strong medium-sized corp that will com-
plement our present configuration," Kuroshima said to
a small crowd of medians. "We have filed notice of
takeover intent with the Consortium in Zurich, and will
begin the offer process on April thirtieth, the earliest
legal date. I'm speaking for myself as well as Flanders
Corp when I say that we sincerely hope our offer will be
accepted in a positive and realistic spirit by Intertel
stockholders and execs."

Bonny reappeared, looking serious. "Our reaction
has been prompt. At the main office in Sydney, Chairman Claudio Chang issued a strong statement."

There was Chang, looking plump, cool, and dangerous despite his lace collar. "Intertel," he said in his
calm Oxford accent, "will resist takeover with all the
means available to us under Consortium law. We are
too important to the world economy to be plundered by
Flanders or anyone else. Our board is confident that our
stockholders will think first of their responsibilities to
eighteen million Intertel members, and will summarily
reject any offer from Flanders."

One of the medians recording him asked Chang,
"Does 'all the means available' mean you're prepared
to use violence to stop this bid?"

"I said 'all the means,' and I meant it. Flanders will
certainly use all means to take us over, if their record
means anything. We expect to call up our Security
Reserves very soon."

Perkin shut off the plate and stared at the Japanese

print on the far wall of his office. War. Like Zeiss and
Michelin. Like Da Han and Singapore Instruments. A
war of psychological pressure, propaganda, corruption,
economic subversion, and unpredictable violence, all
aimed at compelling the other side's execs and stockholders to give in. One stockholder might be bribed;
another assassinated with his or her whole family. A key
factory, staffed by millions of dollars' worth of robots,
might be bombed, or a mall housing thousands of patrons might be poison-gassed.

His mind raced. Intertel's resources were considerable, but everything depended on morale at the top. If
the stockholders thought that they could benefit more
—much more—by rejecting Flanders' bid, the takeover
would fail no matter how much blood had been shed.
And Chang was right about the polydendronic computer. Jethro's design was relatively cheap; Intertel could
mark its computers up by a hundred percent and still
hold a huge, insatiable market. Not just prosthetics: implanted animals could perform jobs too dangerous for
valuable robots, without long and expensive training.
Mental cases could be controlled if not cured outright.
Ordinary people could interface directly with major
computer systems and infonets, or just give themselves
any kind of electronic hallucination they liked. The
gamer market alone would absorb millions of units.
Eventually—say within ten years—the need for surgical
implants would be overcome, and anyone could use a
polydendronic.

The stockholders would risk worse than snipers to
hold on to such a prize. But first it would have to be
tested, demonstrated, proved successful. Thank God
for Chang's prescience and insight; the two million
extra dollars were already working, giving the project an
extra push. Perkins too, would have to push harder
—push himself, his staff, and the experimental subjects.
The staff were loyal Intertel members; they would come
through. Even the subjects would catch the excitement
and do their best.

Only about four weeks until the takeover started. It

could all be over in a month, or two at the outside, unless Intertel's leaders had something to fight for. Perkin looked again at the Japanese print. Almost invisible in a turbulent sea, a boat struggled for shore. Mount Fuji beckoned in the distance. But over the boat hung an enormous, many-horned wave.

That's us, Perkin thought, and felt a shivery elation.

THREE

March 30

"Too bad you missed the TV last night," Gretchen said to Jonathan. It was after lunch; the kids were parked once again by the blue-tiled fountain in the patio while the nannies gossiped in the cool shade of the colonnade.

"It sta-a-ank!" Bobo yelled.

"Put a sock in it, you," Gretchen commanded. Bobo subsided, winking and grimacing at Tran.

"It was all about takeovers," she went on cheerfully. "Did you know somebody's trying to take *us* over? Bonny looked really worried."

He'd seen Bonny many times, of course, but he'd never heard of takeovers until yesterday. He asked Gretchen about them.

"Bonny says it's when one corp buys another corp. They pay the stockholders lots of money, and make 'em stockholders in the first corp. Everybody else has to go, too, but if they don't want you they sell your contract. So you could end up in some corp where you don't even speak the language. If you don't want to go, they make you a patron and you go live in some crummy mall."

"What happens to the nonstats?" Jonathan asked.

"He wants to know what happens to the nonstats," Gretchen interpreted for the others.

Laury swayed in her wheelchair, laughing horribly. "Who cares?"

"Bonny didn't say," Gretchen answered him, ignoring Laury. "I guess they all go with everybody else. No wonder Bonny looked worried. She'd have to go too."

"Bonny isn't a nonstat," Jonathan objected.

"She is! She's a turing, isn't she? Just a bloody computer program, even if she is gorgeous and all. Turings are nonstats, just like us. Only a lot more expensive."

"I like her. She's so pretty," Jonathan muttered. He was shocked; Bonny was one of the people everyone knew, like Captain Nemo and Jethro and Cassandra. They were smart and famous and popular, and lots of people spent money just to be able to talk to them, so how could they be just programs? He began to feel that maybe he wasn't as smart as Gretchen after all.

"Turings are nonstats, lower primates are nonstats, dolphins and whales are nonstats, and defectives are nonstats," Laura chanted.

"Not all defectives," Gretchen snapped. "Not on your life. Lots of kids stay with their parents even if they've got really bad things wrong with them. It's true."

"They're lucky," Tran said softly. "I bet it must be great to have a mother and a father."

"They can have it," Gretchen brayed. "Who wants to be the only cripple in the building? All the other kids give you a lot of stick, buzz you all day long, or act like you're not even there."

"I wouldn't care," Tran murmured. "I'd just be with my mother and father. It'd be great."

"Well, I cared, mate. It was horrible. I was glad when my mum and dad handed me over. I really was glad."

"You mean you weren't a baby?" Jonathan asked.

"Was I a baby, he wants to know. Big bloody baby. I was seven going on eight. Four years after my stroke."

"Do you miss your parents?" Laury asked.

"No chance to. They send me tapes, you know, all the family news. Just like being there. I got a brother now. Four years old—cute little bugger. Good job I'm not there—he'd drive me right 'round the b-bend.''

She fell silent, and Jonathan saw tears in her eyes. He felt sudden anger at her parents. It was one thing to sign you away when you were a baby, and didn't know anything. But a seven-year-old was a person. He imagined himself and Gretchen, both cured, going to Australia to confront her parents. It would be a dramatic scene.

Gretchen didn't say anything more, and Laury took over. "I don't know who my parents were. They got rid of me right away." The others nodded, or tried to. Jonathan tried to contribute his own experiences, but the other kids didn't understand him and Gretchen seemed not to want to translate.

"I was in a crèche in Vermont," Laury went on; she was obviously pleased to have everyone's attention. "It was nice there. It snowed in the winter. But the nurses were mean. Almost as mean as Jane," she added in a whisper.

"Did they talk about you when you were right there?" asked Tran. "They did that to me in L.A. Always calling us names."

"They all do that," Bobo chirped. "They think we're dumb, but they're the dumb ones. We're smart enough. Know what? In the old days kids like us went to school and everything."

"Oh, sure," Laury drawled.

"It's true. My nurse told me."

"Your nursie told you. Oh, your nursie," Laury mocked him. "What did she know? They told me in Vermont that they used to drown vegges."

"No, they didn't!" Bobo shrieked.

"Hey, Bobo, pipe down," Jane warned from the colonnade. "All of you. Talk nice." They obeyed at once; Jonathan suspected that she had socked them all.

"Bobo's right," Gretchen said quietly. "At least I think he is. I heard about vegges being in school too."

"Why?" asked Jonathan. "Why send vegges to school?"

"I dunno."

"Can you find out?"

"What for?" She still seemed sullen and withdrawn.

"For—for finding out. For fun." He sucked at a mouthful of spit. "Do you know about the old days?"

"Not much."

"Was it like on the TV, with the nashies and wars and things?"

"I guess."

"Why did nashies want to put us in school? They were bad guys."

Gretchen looked thoughtful. "I dunno, Jonathan. Doesn't make sense, does it?"

"Can you ask the nannies?"

She snorted. "They wouldn't tell even if they knew." She watched bees in the rosebushes for a time. "If I had a plate—but all I know how to do is get the main channels, so that's no help. But I know where there's books."

"Books?"

"Like in the old shows on TV, you know. They're like a plate made out of paper, and you turn the paper over instead of pressing MORE. There's a room near Dr. Perkin's office, called the library. It's got lots of books. No one ever goes in there."

"Does it have books about spazzes?"

"How should I know until I go in and have a look?"

He had to take a deep breath and make himself relax. "Can you go now?"

"I can try, anyway." She lurched to her feet and limped over to the nannies.

"Can I go to the bathroom?"

"*May* I go. Yes, you may," Judy answered. "Don't take too long." She returned to her conversation with Jane.

A few minutes later Gretchen was back. She sagged onto a bench near Jonathan and murmured, "That was a dead snap. I got two books. One from 1996, the other from 1971. Really old. Guess what—it looked like all the books were about spazzes and brain damage and all that. I couldn't believe it."

"Where are they? The books you got?"

"In my room. I don't know if they'll be any good. The words are hard, and the paper just falls apart. Anyway, I'll see what I can find out." She smiled lopsidedly at him. "Hey, you know, this is fun."

Jonathan smiled.

March 31

On Judy Wong's plate Cassandra looked attentive and sympathetic. The turing's image was that of a black woman, middle-aged and handsome. Today she wore a gold necklace and a frilly white blouse; gold earrings dangled, glittering, against her neck.

"Hi, Cassandra."

"Hi, Judy. How are you? You look a litle upset."

"It shows, huh?"

"It wouldn't to most people. Is it anything you want to talk about?"

"Oh, Cass, gee—I hardly know where to start. The kids bother me, *he* bothers me, the takeover—"

"Hold on." Cassandra chuckled. "The kids bother you, you said."

"They're nice enough, I guess. They can't help being what they are. But I can hardly make myself look at them sometimes. It's—they—they're so horrible."

"Horrible?"

"Crippled. The spastics aren't too bad, except when they try to walk or talk or feed themselves—God, that's really slimy—but that Gretchen never stops dragging herself around. And the new one, the athetoid, he makes my skin crawl. Cass, he just twitches and shudders and drools, and he never quits. I feel like throwing up when I see him, and he's not even housebroken, and I'm the one who usually has to clean him up. Does that make me an awful person?"

"Do you feel like an awful person?"

"I feel kind of helpless. Like I ought to be able to handle it. But I don't want to talk to Jane about it. I *can't* talk to Jane about it. She'd get me transferred."

"You don't want a transfer?"

"I'd feel, you know, like a loser. Besides, if Dr. Perkin's project works, the kids'll be okay soon, and it'll be a big thing to be on his team. I could go anywhere in Intertel." Judy sighed and grinned sheepishly at the turing. "Any advice, Cass?"

"It sounds like Gretchen and Jonathan are the ones who really get to you."

"I think you're right."

"They spend a lot of time together, don't they?"

"Well—sun time and TV time."

"Why not let Gretchen look after him? She can understand him when he talks, and she *can* do quite a bit, you know."

"Like to see her change his diaper with one hand."

"You don't think it's a good idea, then."

"No—no, it's a good idea, Cass."

"Well, try it for a day or two anyway, all right? Put them in the rear patio for sun time, and let Gretchen feed him lunch as well. You won't have to deal with them as much, and you'll be able to do a better job with the other kids. Let me know how it works out."

"Come on, Cass—you can watch them for yourself."

Cassandra grinned and wearily shook her head. "Honey, I have enough to do without all that. I'll rely on your judgment."

"Sure." Judy felt better already.

"Now, who's this 'he' you mentioned?"

"Oh . . . uh, Dr. Perkin. He worries me. He's so intense, so involved in his work. I'm afraid he'll burn himself out."

"Is that the nanny speaking, or the woman?"

Judy laughed self-consciously. "Both. I, uh, kind of have a crush on him, you know? But that's just because, well, he's around and he doesn't have a woman, and I don't have a man."

"That's a very honest insight, Judy. Very perceptive." Cassandra nodded thoughtfully. "Maybe we ought to fix him up with somebody, and fix *you* up with somebody, and you could stop worrying."

"Oh, Cass, bite your tongue!"

"Honey, I'm just teasing. But really, Judy, you're right to say it's just a crush. I mean, he's a Professional-Twelve and you're a Technician-Three. Interstatus romances are okay on the soapers, but you know better."

Judy nodded, feeling a little more mature than she really wanted to be. "Uh-huh."

"Well, there's no law against liking your boss, so go ahead and like him. Just don't like him so much that you quit doing a good job for him."

"Don't you worry about that, Cass. I won't let him down."

"Honey, I know you won't. Say, did I hear you say something about this takeover?"

"Oh, uh-huh, but it's not as serious. I just hate to think about those Flanders jerks holding our contracts."

"It gets to everyone, honey. It's rough, but we'll get through it."

"Do you guys ever think about it?"

"Sure. Heck, honey, I got taken over myself, remember? I used to be with IBM/Sony, just like you. Course, you were just a little girl then. But you know what I've learned? Just working hard is a great way to forget your troubles."

"That's good advice. Look, Cass, I've taken up enough of your time. But thanks. Sometimes I don't know what I'd do without you."

Cassandra grinned, white teeth flashing in her dark face. "Honey, I'm just doing my job, you know, like everyone else, but I always like to talk with you. Call me again soon. And let me know how it works out with Gretchen and Jonathan."

"I sure will."

Reluctantly Judy signed off. Her plate briefly flashed the bill for turing time: fifteen dollars, about two days' pay, and well worth it. She thought fondly about Cassandra. How many thousands of members had she been comforting and consoling at the same time? It didn't matter; when she listened, she seemed to listen to you alone, and her advice was solid, wise, and uncritical.

Bonny was good, too, a sympathetic buddy—like an older sister, especially about man problems. Captain Nemo was great when you needed fatherly encouragement or a fatherly chewing out. Jethro was best for testing your wits against a supersmart kid brother. But Cass —Cass was the mother every girl should have.

April 1

"If I've gotta feed you, you've gotta keep still," Gretchen growled.

"I'm trying to."

They sat in the rear patio, a much smaller open space. Bougainvillea splashed purple over an arched trellis above them, giving shade and privacy. Bamboo rustled in a breeze; parakeets fluttered in out of the sky.

"I read some of what's in those books last night, when I went to the can. Boy, are they hard."

Jonathan swallowed beef paste and worked his tongue into position. "What do they say?"

"In the old days kids like us usually got looked after by their parents. And they got all kinds of training, to make 'em learn to do things. Exercises, you know?"

"Like in the crèche, and here."

"That's just to keep your muscles from tying you up in knots. They used to do exercises so they could *do* things. And listen: they *did* go to school."

"So Bobo was right."

"Not all of 'em, but a lot. Some even learned to drive cars. I mean really drive, on manual, not just telling the car where they wanted to go. They could do all sorts of bloody stuff."

"They must have been smarter than us."

"Bet they weren't, mate. They looked like us. Some looked worse."

"How come we don't go to school, then?"

"I dunno. Yet. Maybe I'll find out when I read some more." She wiped his chin. "Maybe it was automation."

"Why?"

"Well, before they had everything automated, people used to do all kinds of robot jobs, right, just like on TV. That meant they needed lots of people, so they must've even needed spazzes to help. Then when the robots came in, people could relax and do whatever they felt like."

"Like patrons?"

"Yeah. So then they didn't need spazzes, and nobody wanted to look after 'em or teach 'em things. After feeding you your lunch, I can see why too." He knew she was teasing, and refused to rise to the bait, so she went on. "Besides, there's hardly any of us. Hardly worth the trouble."

"Then why did we come here?"

"I told you, didn't I? They just look at us to see what went wrong. Same with the animals."

"What animals?"

Her eyes sparkled. "I'll show you."

Gretchen pushed him down deserted corridors and through a heavy door into a wide concrete-floored yard shaded by the building. Within a concrete-block wall topped with barbed wire stood rows of cages. All but three were empty. In one a big dog trotted restlessly; across from him two chimpanzees rocked back and forth, each on one foot.

"The dog's name is Buck. He can't see anything, and I don't think he can hear either. The chimps are Plato and Darwin. They look like they've had strokes. See, Plato stays on his right foot and Darwin stays on his left, and they only use one arm."

Strong, sour odors filled the yard. Buck paced back and forth, his yellow-brown eyes clear but unseeing. His pink tongue lolled in the heat. He paused and sniffed the air, whining a little.

"He smells us," Jonathan said. "Push me closer."

"He might bite."

"No, he won't."

Reluctantly Gretchen put his wheelchair alongside the cage. Jonathan hooked two fingers in the wire mesh. Buck sniffed his hand, then licked it. Jonathan gurgled with delight.

"He likes me! He likes me!" His restless fingers scratched randomly over the dog's muzzle and settled on an ear. Buck leaned blissfully against the wire, letting Jonathan rub and scratch. Jonathan had never patted a dog before; the feel and scent of fur were strange and pleasant.

Gretchen, once she saw the dog was harmless, limped across to the chimpanzees.

"Plato's like me," she said. "Right, mate? Got a bum right brain." The chimps ignored her, each rocking to his own rhythm, each with a paralyzed leg curled under him. She watched them for a moment; then she noticed the new scars on their scalps.

"What's this, then? You had your heads cut open? I didn't notice that before." She went back to Jonathan. "Guess what. Those chimps didn't have strokes. I'll bet they got cut open. Look at Buck."

The scar ran right around the dog's skull, from one ear to the other. Jonathan had felt it, but assumed it was a normal part of the dog.

"We'd better get back, before they come looking for us," Gretchen said. "And listen—don't tell the other kids about the animals, all right? Don't want them spoiling a good thing."

They were back in the cool, dim corridors. Jonathan said, "They cut the animals' brains open, didn't they?"

"Guess so." She quickened her uneven steps.

"Why?"

"Beats me. Makes me kind of nervous, though."

"Gretchen, are they going to cut our brains?"

She laughed. "Whatever for, mate? We're already bunged up, aren't we?"

"Maybe they'll bung us up some more."

"Hey, make up your mind—are they gonna cure us or cut us open?"

"I don't know. I'm not so sure now." They were nearing the big patio. "Tomorrow, tell me more about spazzes in the old days."

"Wow—make me work." She tousled his hair; he chuckled.

April 7

Captain Nemo looked like a tall, saturnine man of forty-five or fifty. Dark hair streaked with gray fell across his high forehead; his eyes were deep-set, a sharp blue. A close-trimmed beard softened the hard line of his jaw. Tonight he was dressed with the somber elegance of thirty or forty years before: a black coat over an ivory-colored shirt with an upturned collar and a ruby brooch at his throat.

"Good evening, Dr. Perkin, Phil." The turing's voice was deep and resonant. Both men unconsciously sat up straighter.

"Good evening, Captain," Perkin replied. "Thank you for answering so promptly. I'm calling about the prototypes."

"Of course. The first three are completed and debugged. They will be in your hands tomorrow morning."

"Wonderful! I—I thought it would take another week."

"You did say you wanted them urgently."

"Any problems?"

"None. It is a good design."

"Excuse me, Captain—" Phil Haddad spoke up. "I've been thinking about Jethro's design. It seems to have an awful lot of unused memory capacity."

Captain Nemo smiled faintly. "So does a baby, Phil. Don't forget that the computer will be receiving information from three sources: Intertel's central computer, the subject's sensory input, and the subject's own memory. Redundancy is as essential for the computer as for the host brain."

"Even so, Captain, I—"

"The printouts carry a more detailed rationale," Captain Nemo said. Phil subsided. Captain Nemo was Intertel's oldest turing, created by IBM/Sony early in the century and acquired in the takeover by Intertel seventeen years before. If Jethro was the master designer, Captain Nemo was the master builder; few questioned him, let alone argued with him.

"Do you have any advice on the implant procedure, now that the computers are ready?" Perkin asked.

"I've reviewed your plans; they're very detailed, and I see nothing to criticize."

High praise; Perkin suppressed a flattered smile. "You're very welcome to monitor the implantations."

"One of us will, I am sure."

"Very good. . . . Captain Nemo, may I change the subject?"

"Of course."

"Have you heard anything new on the takeover?"

"No."

"Has Flanders been doing anything that might be part of the takeover?"

"We've had two attemps by Trojan-horse programs to break into the central computer. They were fairly sophisticated, so we assume they were done by Flanders' turings. Neither attempt came near succeeding. Otherwise everything has been very quiet."

"Are the stockholders taking protective measures?"

Captain Nemo, smiling, shook his head. "I'm not authorized to comment on stockholders. You understand."

"Of course." A tactful rebuff; he had been reminded of his status. "Well, we won't take any more of your time. I'm delighted that the computer is ready so soon. We'll go ahead with the implants tomorrow afternoon. I hope you'll be watching."

"As I said, one of us will observe. Until then."

He faded from the screen. Perkin and Phil avoided each other's eyes.

"He's smart, all right," said Phil. "But he doesn't

understand people. He always makes me feel stupid."

"That's why turings are nonstats." Perkin looked at the Japanese wave on his wall. "They're very smart, and they know a lot, but they don't know enough. Better said, they don't understand."

"That's it, Dr. Perkin. That's it exactly. They know, but they don't understand."

The TV hour before dinner had a regular pattern. The nannies brought the kids in from their rooms or tests, parked them in the basement recreation room, and adjourned to the staff lounge next door. The rec room TV wall was always tuned to Channel 8, Intertel's infonet for children and patrons.

Today the show was an adventure documentary, starting off with a story about the first bubble walkers in the Aleutian trench. They were three young Intertel stockholders, two handsome men and a lovely woman, who smiled at each other while the support team aboard their hoveryacht prepared their equipment. Jonathan had seen it before; they all had, but Bobo and Tran watched as attentively as ever while the others yawned and wiggled.

"Why do they always show the same stuff on TV?" Laury wondered.

"It's free," answered Gretchen. "No commercials, just the corporate-service plugs. The stuff on the other infonets is new, but you gotta pay for it."

"How come *you* know so much, smarty?" Laury snapped.

" 'Cause my parents are professionals. My mum used to explain it all to me."

"*Your* parents were pro*fes*sionals. La-de-dah. You must get bored with us."

"Yeah, sometimes. Hey, Jonathan, I read something interesting this morning. They used to think brain-damaged kids would disappear. In the 1996 book, it says they could tell when a kid was gonna have trouble even before he was born. Then they'd do operations to help."

"Well, they were wrong," said Jonathan. "There's a lot of us still around."

"Yeah," said Gretchen.

"If you two are gonna talk," said Laury, "you could at least tell me what he's saying. And what's this book?"

"It's an old book about cerebral palsy. I've been reading it. And guess what? They didn't drown vegges in the old days. They went to school, like Bobo said."

"Yay for Bobo," said Bobo. Laury looked away, then turned back.

"What else did the book say?"

On TV the three adventurers reached the bottom of the trench. Their force bubble barely cleared their heads; they walked awkwardly on the bottom of the bubble, a few centimeters above the gray ooze of the sea floor. Strange fish circled them, glittering in the floodlights; the explorers' breaths were frosty white, and they seemed cold even in their parkas and heavy trousers.

"Vegges could do all kinds of things. They could drive cars, and swim, and run those bonky old computers they had back then. Some of 'em even wrote books."

"Aw, that's all a story." Laury swung herself back to watch the TV. The bubble walkers were rising again, back toward the sunlight high above.

Jonathan tried to regain the thread of the conversation while the TV flashed into a popular adventure series about the victory of the Consortium over the nashies. The actor playing Gilbert Russell was at an old-fashioned computer terminal, stealthily getting into a nashie computer in a stronghold called the Pentagon. "We're still around," said Jonathan. "Nobody taught us—"

"My parents taught *me,*" Gretchen interrupted.

"I mean us crèche kids. They exercised us so we wouldn't bend our bodies too much, and they let us watch TV. But we don't *do* anything. What do vegges do when they grow up?"

Gretchen looked at him blankly. "I don't know. I

never saw any older than fifteen or sixteen, like us.''

"Maybe they send them to places like this, and make them better.''

"Then why don't they tell us that? All they ever say is 'We need to do more tests, dear.' '' She watched a nashie general sneak up behind Gilbert Russell and shoot him. Blood spurted out of Russell's arm onto the computer screen. "I better go look at some more books.''

"Make the nannies tell you.''

"I told you, spaz—they don't answer. I used to pester the daylights out of 'em. I always thought they figured I wouldn't understand. Now—maybe they think I'd understand, all right, and they don't want me to.'' Her eyes darkened.

Bobo, who had been lying on a beanbag chair watching the screen, suddenly stiffened. His legs jutted; his arms waved in tight little circles. Only the whites of his eyes showed, and he made choking noises.

"Bloody hell,'' Gretchen shouted. She yelled for the nannies as she limped over to the boy and flopped down beside him. Reaching into his mouth, she pulled his tongue out of his throat.

Jane and Judy fluttered in, saying nothing, and lifted Bobo up in their arms. "Good girl, Gretchen,'' said Judy. "Poor old Bobo—one convulsion after another. We better get Dr. Perkin to look at his dosages again.''

"Another few days and it won't matter,'' Jane answered quietly.

They carried Bobo out while Laury and Tran watched. Jonathan glanced at Gretchen, still sprawled on the carpet. She was watching the nannies leave, and her face held an expression of mixed anger and fear.

Why won't it matter? Jonathan wondered, but he didn't ask it aloud. He was too scared to.

FOUR

April 8

Two rows of seats encircled the operating theater. Most of the seats were empty, but a few staff members were present, as well as three medians: one from Intertel, one from Irancor, and one from Independent News. All three were young women wearing stereo caps; the twin lenses on their foreheads reminded Perkin of spiders' eyes.

"Good morning," he said to them from the floor of the theater. "Today we will be implanting computers of radically new design in three experimental subjects." He gestured to the tables behind him, where Buck, Darwin, and Plato lay tranquilized. "I will be commenting during the operations, but I'll try to keep it simple and nontechnical. The medical and engineering details will be available tomorrow on Intertel Infonet Twelve."

Perkin nodded to the surgical teams, who applied neuronic blocks to the three animals.

"I'll be supervising the operations, but feel free to ask me questions at any time," he said with a smile to the medians. They smiled back; their lenses glinted under the operating-room lights.

While his surgeons opened the animals' skulls, Perkin explained how each subject had been function-impaired. By patching into the overhead cameras, the medians were able to record each step of the procedures. The brains lay exposed, gleaming wetly. Perkin pointed out the lesions and described the effects they had caused.

"And here we have the polydendronic computers." Perkin walked over to an aluminum trolley holding three cylindrical containers. "These are synthetic-protein biochemical models, with a newly designed circuit. You could almost say they've been grown instead of built. Once implanted, they'll extend their dendrons into different regions of the brain and take over the lost functions."

"How long will that take, Dr. Perkin?" asked the Japanese woman from Independent.

"About two days—maybe less. It takes very little time for the computer to orient itself and determine which brain areas to occupy."

"So it's programmed already?"

"In part, yes. But it will also self-program from the host's brain tissue, very much like a—" He caught himself as he was about to say "zombie button." That was not the analogy to make. "Like a kind of cerebral pacemaker. And we can add more programming by inductance field, or even by old-fashioned wiring."

He carried the first cylinder to the team working on Buck. The surgeon withdrew the computer from its warm, moist nest and held it in the palm of his hand so that the medians could zoom in on it.

"As you can see, the core unit is about the size and shape of an almond," Perkin said. "The eight main dendrons are almost invisible. But they'll extend and branch to an aggregate length of over twenty meters. All right, Doctor, go ahead."

The surgeon gently placed the core between the two halves of Buck's brain. Pinkish-brown, the computer looked very much like a living organ.

"The screen behind us monitors the computer's status," said Perkin. "As you can see, all three are now in inactive mode. I'll command the dog's implant to go active." Standing at a console beside the screen, Perkin stroked a keyboard. The screen showed a translucent green image of Buck's brain, with an orange ovoid—the implant—resting upon it. Below the image, bright-blue numbers and letters began to flicker in orderly rows.

"All right." Perkin realized how tense he had become only when he began to relax. "The implant is functioning normally and beginning to anchor itself. The subject is responding well. No changes in respiration, blood pressure, brain activity, or immune responses. We'll attach the antenna node and close him up. Thank you, Doctor," he said to the surgeon.

The median from Irancor spoke up. "Dr. Perkin, how does this differ from any ordinary prosthetic computer?"

"In effect, by becoming part of the brain. An ordinary biochemical prosthetic interfaces with, say, the nerve endings in a severed limb. The user can command the artificial limb and does receive some sensory input from it. But that interface is almost useless if the brain itself is damaged. Polydendronics will almost surely find some uses in standard prosthetics, but they'll be most useful in people whose limbs are sound but whose nervous systems are not. They'll also enable us to program animals for complex tasks." He patted Darwin's hairy shoulder. The chimp, deep in the trance of the neuronic block, did not move.

"This fellow here, for example, could be put to more challenging work than chimps are normally capable of, where it's not worth building a sufficiently agile robot."

"Won't that still be pretty expensive?" asked the median from Intertel.

"In mass production these computers will cost under two thousand dollars apiece, including implant and basic programming. A young chimp could work for fifteen years or more for half the cost of a comparable robot. Even including bananas," he added with a boyish smile.

"So this could be a very profitable innovation for Intertel?" asked the woman from Independent.

Perkin nodded, still smiling. The question had

sounded very natural and unrehearsed; and of course it had to come from her instead of from the Intertel median, who was expected to flack for her own corp.

"Very profitable indeed, I believe. But more than profitable. We see it as the basis of a major new industry, comparable to the automobile or the inductance field. And personally, I see it as an undreamed-of blessing to countless people whose lives will be wonderfully changed by the polydendronic computer."

They already had a thirty-second cassette, compiled by Captain Nemo with voice-overs by Bonny and Cassandra, on the benefits of the new computer: running children, old people stepping out of wheelchairs, gymnasts whirling over rings and bars. It was all graphies, generated by the turings, and so labeled as the law required; but it had the slightly grainy look of "real" video. The turings were past masters of PR.

After a few more questions Perkin turned back to oversee the closing steps of the operations. Everything went very smoothly. The chimps were brought up to twilight sleep, then to the edge of consciousness; they signed fuzzily to each other as their wheelchairs took them out. Buck whined a little as his neuronic block was lifted. His surgeon patted him reassuringly, and the dog allowed himself to be picked up and put on the floor.

"Everything's looking good," Perkin said, chuckling to the medians. "And Buck will be looking 'real good' by the weekend."

The young women tittered at his play on words; it was based on patron dialect, and for a professional it was on the borderline between wit and bad taste. Perkin didn't care. They'd edit it out anyway, to close with the shot of the German shepherd tamely walking out on a leash held by a nurse.

"Really good stuff," said Irancor's median. "We'll give it good play. Dr. Perkin, I want a reserved seat when you do the nonstat kids. You'll have more coverage than you ever dreamed of."

"You three will have front-row seats, I assure you."

He strode lightly from the operating theater, through the cool, dim corridors to his office. In the morning light the mountain looked very close and Flanders seemed very far away.

April 11

    "Well, the king and queen," said Laury sarcastically, her fingers twisted around the arms of her wheelchair. "Welcome, your highnesses."

Gretchen pushed Jonathan into his usual place in the rec room and flopped onto a couch without answering. The other kids had been teasing them ever since Gretchen had taken over Jonathan's lunch. Lately, with fewer tests, their whole afternoons had been free; Jonathan had learned to read a lot of words, and they had talked for hours at a time. It helped to make up for all the needling they got when they rejoined the others.

Tran and Bobo were rolling on the floor, tickling and pinching each other. The TV screen showed a soaper: A well-dressed exec couple were speaking softly, intently, on the balcony of an Alpine chalet. The woman was weeping. The man stroked her tawny hair and murmured in her ear.

"Don't bother to say hello," Laury went on. "You must've had a lovely lunch and afternoon with just each other."

"Lo-o-o-ve bi-irds," Bobo gurgled. Tran swung at him with one rigid arm, meaning to tickle, but hitting Bobo in the face. "Ow! You—"

"All right, all of you quit it," Gretchen said quietly and grimly. The younger boys stopped yelling and rolled over to gape at her. Laury pretended to be watching the soaper.

"Get this," Gretchen continued. "We didn't ask to be put together. That was Judy's idea. And if you think it's a treat to feed old Jonathan, you're welcome to it. But listen . . ."

They responded to the drop in her voice, turning away from the soaper. Sitars twanged as the exec lovers nuzzled each other, now on a houseboat in Kashmir.

"We've been going to see the animals. Buck and Darwin and Plato. Remember, I told you about them? Well, a few days ago we couldn't get into their yard. It was full of people. We heard somebody say they'd had implants."

"What's implants?" Bobo asked.

"Like a machine in your body. Remember that soaper where the girl got a new heart? That's an implant."

"Oh."

"So what?" Laury drawled.

"We heard somebody say, 'The kids are next.' *We're* gonna get implants."

"Are they gonna cut us?"

"Yes."

"Have we got bad hearts?"

"It's not just hearts, Bobo. Buck and the chimps are all bunged up like us. Maybe their implants are to fix 'em up again, and maybe we'll get fixed up too."

"So we can walk and everything?" Laury's eyes widened.

"I was right!" Jonathan crowed. "I told her they were going to help us."

"What? What's he saying?" Tran asked. Gretchen translated. Tran looked at Jonathan with surprised respect. "He must be smart after all."

"Judy! Jane!" Bobo screamed. The nannies came through the door, looking annoyed.

"What is it now?" Jane demanded.

"Are we gonna get implants? In our heads?"

"What in the world makes you think that?"

"Gretchen and Jonathan said so," Laury said.

"Oh, did they? Well, let's not get ahead of ourselves. We'll just wait and see, okay? Now—time for supper. TV off. Gretchen, you feed Jonathan again." She glanced at Judy. "How do they find these things out? Did you tell them?"

"Certainly not!"

Jonathan laughed his *uh-uh-uh;* Gretchen, pushing his wheelchair, tweaked his earlobe.

April 12

Buck sat on the concrete floor of the animal yard and watched Duane Perkin. The German shepherd's brown eyes were focused; he grinned, tongue lolling in the desert heat.

"Buck—come."

The dog sprang to his feet and trotted lightly to him. Perkin patted his head.

"Sit. Stay." Perkin threw a stick, clattering, down the yard. "Fetch."

Buck raced to the wall, took up the stick, and trotted proudly back with it.

Phil Haddad, sitting on a bench behind Perkin, chuckled and thumped his fist on the wood. "He can see and hear. He can do it."

"So far so good. This is only the fifth day."

"He was as blind and deaf as a scalpel could make him, and now he's focusing, tracking, echolocating—the works."

Perkin nodded, smiling, and threw the stick again. Buck sprang away. "Come and see the chimps," Perkin said.

With Buck following, they walked across the yard to the chimp cages. Plato and Darwin were sitting up, fingers hooked in the wire mesh, watching the men. Their shaved scalps already showed a faint stubble.

"No more rocking back and forth," Perkin observed. "They limp a little, and they favor one hand or the other. But that'll change as muscle tone improves." He fished in a pocket of his slacks and brought out a couple of sugar cubes. Darwin and Plato grunted and extended their hands through the mesh.

"Other hand," he commanded. Each chimp put out the hand that had been paralyzed; each accepted a sugar cube and closed his fingers around it. Darwin popped his cube into his mouth; Plato fumbled his, but used the same hand to retrieve it.

"That's marvelous, Dr. Perkin. They should be ready for post-op checkout and debugging by tomorrow."

"They'll be all yours. I don't think you'll find any unpleasant surprises."

"How long before you sacrifice them?"

Perkin thought for a few seconds. "It's almost more of a political decision than a medical one. They make good tape while they're running around, and we need all the publicity we can get."

"Any stockholder feedback yet?"

"Some, mostly positive. But the support is from the people you'd expect, like the Akutagawas and the Kennedys. They're against the takeover no matter what. It's the pragmatists who worry me. They're keeping very quiet."

"When they see our little twitch-heads doing cartwheels, they'll change their minds."

Perkin nodded but did not look happy. "Buck and the chimps are okay as PR, but the infonets are treating them as curiosities. That means the kids have to come through big—dramatic improvement, cartwheels, that sort of thing. If anything goes wrong with them, Buck can chase sticks for the rest of his life and it won't make any difference."

They walked Buck back to his cage and locked him in.

"All the more reason to sacrifice the animals soon," said Phil, "and spot any trouble before the kids get their implants."

"Maybe. . . . We'll keep an eye on the animals. Anything odd or unexpected, and we'll open 'em up. Otherwise we'll keep them alive until next week, after the kids' turn."

*   *   *

April 17

The median was a tall blonde in a suit of gray satin and white lace. Jonathan met her first, during the morning's tests; she taped him for a few minutes, chatted with the technicians, and left.

"More PR," said Gretchen at lunch. She and Jonathan were in the rear patio, as usual. "She taped all of us with those dumb goggles on her head. Did she talk to you?"

"Talked *about* me." He slurped lemonade through a straw. "She asked the techs how old I was. How smart I was. They said, 'About average.' My IQ is one thirty-five. But you know what? She asked when we were getting our implants, and they said tomorrow."

"Day after—God. It's really gonna happen?"

"Uh-uh-uh." Jonathan sucked spit off his lower lip. "Gretchen? Will it hurt?"

"I don't think so. Even if it does—who cares, if we can walk and run and use both our hands?"

"I know . . . I just get tired of hurting all the time. Be nice not to hurt. Like being asleep only awake, I guess. Gretchen, if we get fixed up, will you still like me?"

"Why shouldn't I?"

" 'Cause you're so smart and pretty. You'll be able to do anything. If you go to school you'll be way ahead of me and I'll never catch up."

"Get away!" She looked flattered and embarrassed and a little guilty. "You just told me how smart you are, didn't you? Anyway, you're my friend, and my friends stay my friends. Understand?"

Jonathan wanted to say "I love you" but knew how it would sound, mumbling out of his contorted mouth.

"Anyway, Jonathan, you'll catch up right away. I know you will."

He could tell she meant it, and loved her all the more.

"Know what I wish?" Gretchen asked absently, watching the parakeets flutter about the patio. "I wish we could learn everything in the world, all at once, and go on learning. Wouldn't that be wonderful, knowing

everything and not being so bloody pig-ignorant?''
    ''Yes, yes.''

        After dinner that evening Jane and Judy
brought the kids back into the rec room. As a special
treat they were being allowed to watch the blond median's report on them and the Center.
    It was part of a newscast on an outside infonet; ac-
cording to Jane, millions around the world watched it.
It looked different to Jonathan: the announcers were
dressed more soberly than Bonny usually was, and they
were probably humans. Most of the newcasts he'd ever
seen had been for Intertel patrons, and he suspected that
this infonet was aimed at an upstatus audience; it
seemed somehow more grown-up.
    The show began with a report on a meeting of Con-
sortium leaders in a city called Bern. More interesting to
Jonathan and the others was the opening of the British
Parliament, whatever that was; it involved lots of horse-
men in polished breastplates, and King Harold and
Queen Ingrid waving from a carriage. He'd seen them
before, but had always thought they were the rulers of
Canada, not of Britain. He would have to ask Gretchen
about it.
    ''A California lab owned by Intertel is experimenting
on disabled children,'' the announcer said gravely.
''With details, Michiko Gunnarson.''
    The blond woman stood in the entry courtyard of the
Center, outlining its purposes. Jonathan knew the
woman herself had taped the scene, and a computer had
later superimposed a graphie image of her.
    ''There's Bobo!'' Laury shrieked. Everyone shushed
her. Michiko Gunnarson asked an unseen attendant a
few questions while Bobo lurched from his bed to a
wheelchair. Glimpses followed of the others, sometimes
with Jane or Judy or another tech in the background.
    ''Here's our most hopeless case,'' Jane was saying as
Jonathan's image filled the screen. Light glinted on a
strand of spittle between his chin and his chest. His
hands slapped and writhed against the armrests of his

wheelchair. His face broke into meaningless grins and grimaces. Jonathan felt his skin prickle; the screen seemed to retreat to the end of a long tunnel. "He's fifteen years old, but he has no more coordination than a six-week-old baby. We figure Dr. Perkin and his team will really be doing something if they can help this one."

She hadn't said those things when the median had taped him. His face burned with shame at the sight of himself, blown up to three times life-size in 3-D.

Suddenly the image was that of Buck trotting across the exercise yard.

"A few days ago this dog was deaf and blind," the median was saying. "Now he can see and hear fairly well. Results have encouraged Dr. Perkin to move on to tests on these nonstat children."

They saw a tall, gray-haired man standing in an operating theater, speaking silently. It must be Dr. Perkin; none of the kids had ever seen him.

"If he's lucky, the children will recover at least some use of their crippled bodies and brains. It's a promising development, though much work lies ahead before it can be marketed. But the attendant who talked about 'helping' these children wasn't entirely accurate. Dr. Perkin's experimental animals and children will have to be sacrificed—killed so that autopsies can show how well the computer implants have adapted to their hosts." The image of Dr. Perkin broke into silent laughter. "It's perfectly legal, of course," Michiko Gunnarson continued, "but many people of all statuses see such treatment of experimental subjects as controversial."

"Turn that thing off!" shouted Jane. "Turn that bitch off right now." The TV obediently went blank.

Tran started crying, a high-pitched bleat. Bobo heaved himself out of his chair and staggered for the door. He smelled of urine.

"Gonna kill us! Gonna kill us!" Laury howled. "Jonathan was wrong! I dowanna! I dowanna! *Maamaaa!*"

*   *   *

A few minutes later the children, all heavily tranquilized, were in their cribs. The nannies stood in Perkin's office, heads bowed. A brilliant sunset filled the office with golden light.

"Of course she was a Flanders plant," Perkin said tightly. "We screwed this one up totally—no, not you girls, it's my responsibility. Now the kids are so juiced on adrenaline, we'll have a devil of a time rebalancing their chemistries by tomorrow morning. . . . Christ, Jane, how could you be so foolish? Who brought up the sacrifice angle?"

"She did, the median. I tried to change the subject, I really did—" Her voice was breaking. "Oh, Dr. Perkin, I'm so sorry."

"Quit. The damage is done. It's really unfair, though. Any research group that uses nonstats is bound to sacrifice some of them, but who makes a fuss? At least they die to help others. But every half-wit with a little status thinks it's wrong. Not that they'd like to go back to rats and rabbits and dying old at seventy. Hypocrites. . . . Okay. They're trying to hurt our image, soften us up for the takeover. We won't oblige them. When the world sees those kids walking and running, we'll get public opinion solidly back on our side."

"What about s-sacrificing?" Judy whispered.

"No sacrifice of animals or nonstats is contemplated. Period. Understood? That's what you'll tell the media. That's what you'll tell the kids too. And make 'em believe it. If you can't calm them down, you're not doing your jobs. Understood?"

"Yes, sir," they murmured together.

"All right. The implants are still scheduled for ten thirty tomorrow. We'll have an Intertel median on hand, and one from Independent, and one from Irancor. No one else. Have the kids ready and prepared: rested, calm, heads shaved."

"Yes, sir," they repeated. Then they left, silently.

Perkin looked at the flaming sunset above the mountain. His plate blinked and beeped with an incoming call. He punched it into recording mode; let the media vultures wait. Instead of recording, though, the screen brightened and the face of Claudio Chang appeared.

"Dr. Perkin, good evening. Excuse me for overriding and barging in like this."

"Good evening, Chairman. Please excuse *me*, sir, for blocking your call."

"Quite all right, I assure you." Chang smiled. "In your place, I would be grateful for a moment's peace after that broadcast."

"I must apologize for that, Chairman. I should have screened that Gunnarson woman before giving her access."

"When you love a project, when you believe in it, it's hard to imagine that others don't. I don't blame you, Dr. Perkin. Better to be too trusting than too suspicious."

Perkin found himself shivering with gratitude and admiration for Chang's understanding, and did not trust himself to speak.

"This was one of their opening shots," Chang went on. "Flanders is finding our range. You're not the only target."

"We'll tighten security at once, Chairman."

"No, leave that to me. You look after your work. I promise you, Flanders won't get near your Center again."

"Thank you . . . very much, sir."

"A good exec looks after his people, especially when they're doing vital work. Keep it up, Dr. Perkin."

"Yes, sir."

"And don't worry about this Gunnarson woman. The fuss will blow over, especially once you get those children on their feet."

"I'm sure, Chairman."

"It must be a real challenge, keeping such defectives alive even under ideal circumstances. What with the trauma of an experimental surgical technique, the mortality rate could be depressing."

"Yes, sir." Perkin felt his spirits lift. Chang understood, and had given his blessing.

"Thank you for your time, Dr. Perkin. It's encouraging to know the project is in responsible hands. Good evening." He vanished from the screen.

Perkin drew a deep breath and let it out again. Back in the national centuries, when wars had been commonplace, men had often gone off to battle in joy, in exhilaration. To a corp-reared, peace-loving man like himself, such emotions had always seemed bizarre, foolish, even demented. Now he understood them properly, for he felt them.

Holding his hand over the desk, he studied his fingers closely. They were steady, relaxed, and strong. The muscles of his wrist and forearm did not move.

He called his chief surgeon, and cut off the man's commiseration about the newscast.

"Never mind all that. We're doing the kids tomorrow morning, as scheduled. I'll be on the team."

FIVE

April 18

Jonathan woke slowly and incompletely, feeling rested and calm, and found himself strapped in a wheeled bed. It was being pushed by two orderlies down one of the dim corridors. He decided it was all right, and then realized they must have tranquilized him during the uproar after the news last night. He felt the way he had during the flight from Vancouver.

Unable to move his head, he listened: several beds must be moving in line down the corridor. Someone muttered sleepily; it sounded like Bobo. *They're going to do it to all of us,* Jonathan decided, and wished he could see Gretchen.

The air was sharp with unfamiliar smells, and at the corners of his vision he glimpsed strange figures standing at intervals along the walls. They wore mirror helmets that hid their faces, and equally reflective cuirasses: Security guards, in antilaser armor, just like in the zappers on TV.

Maybe they're afraid of us, Jonathan thought, and smiled at the idea. Then he remembered what had been on TV the night before and twitched against his straps. Why would they need all these guys to kill a few kids? Everything was crazy.

The bed turned to the right, through two close-set

doorways, and into a room glaringly bright. He squinted against the light and was aware of a large space filled with people. Their rustle and murmur died down. Someone stroked his forehead, and Jonathan realized his head had been shaved smooth. He shouted for Gretchen.

"Jonathan," she answered sleepily. She was close by, yet he could not move to see her.

"I love you," he called out to her.

Then something cold touched his neck, and he relaxed into a dark, still numbness. Far away he heard a man say, "All right, let's begin. Please keep a camera on each subject."

By mid-afternoon it was all over. The children were sleeping in their rooms; the surgical team had left; the medians were gone. Perkin, keyed up after hours of concentration, sat alone and tense in his office, monitoring the kids. Then he got up and prowled down the cool corridors to the light and heat of the animal yard.

Less than five minutes later Phil Haddad was there as well, summoned by Perkin's ring-mike.

"Look at Buck," Perkin said coldly.

The big German shepherd was staggering between two rows of cages, his legs stiff and clumsy. Perkin threw a stick; it landed at Buck's feet, but he only bumped his muzzle when he tried to pick it up. Then he flopped onto his side, breathing erratically.

"Look at the chimps," said Perkin.

Darwin and Plato were trying to feed themselves from their chow troughs, but their hands twitched and shuddered, scattering chow pellets. Darwin shifted his weight and fell on his back. It took him some time to regain his feet.

"Call for some techs," Perkin ordered. "I want the implants monitored."

"The turings warned us there'd be some disorientation," Phil said.

"Ten days later? And so bad that they're worse off than they were before?" Perkin's voice was tight with anger. "Get them into the lab and inside an inductance field. If I find so much as an alpha wave out of place, I'm cutting them open on the spot. And get Captain Nemo to observe," he added, striding out of the yard.

In Lab A, the animals sat half conscious in cages, dulled by a signal to their implants. First Buck's implant, then Darwin's, then Plato's, was interrogated by the central computer, using a weak inductance field. The readouts flickered colorfully across several screens and plates.

"Where's Captain Nemo?" Perkin snapped, looking up from a profile of Darwin's cortical activity.

"I keep getting a temporary hold when I try to access him."

"Hell. Call Jethro."

"I did. Temporary hold. Uh, Dr. Perkin—I can't access Buck's implant memory."

"Why not?"

"No response to commands."

Perkin stopped and looked off across the carpeted expanse of the lab. Then he ordered the central computer to display the animals' records for the last three days. Everything looked normal: They had been eating, exercising, and sleeping normally, and their twice-daily monitoring in the inductance field had shown nothing unusual.

"Remember what Captain Nemo told us the other day, about the raids on the central computer? He figured it was Flanders' turings behind the raids. Maybe they tried again, got at the computer while the animals were linked up to it through the inductance field—"

"No, no." Realizing how brusquely he was speaking to a Professional-12, Phil cleared his throat. "It, uh, doesn't seem likely, Dr. Perkin. I know what our defenses are like. I suspect we've just got a glitch; we'll solve it. —Whoops, here we go! Got access."

Perkin suppressed a sarcastic comment. His nerves must be getting to him if he was sharing his anxieties with underlings.

"Looks perfectly okay, Dr. Perkin . . . everything

looks good." Phil thought for a moment, then ordered the central computer to release Buck from his dulled state. The dog stood up, shook himself, sat down, and gazed out of his cage at the two men. His tail thumped.

"He doesn't have the staggers anymore," Perkin murmured. His plate chimed, and Captain Nemo appeared on the screen.

"My apologies, gentlemen. Is something the matter with the animals?"

"Something *was*," Perkin answered. "They were severely disoriented, and we couldn't get adequate access to the implants. Suddenly everything cleared up."

"I can see that Buck appears normal, and his telemetry confirms it. What about the chimpanzees? Can you rouse them?"

Perkin did so; Darwin and Plato yawned and smacked their lips.

"No problems," said Captain Nemo. "All their responses are normal."

"Captain, I can't have this. I want to know what happened."

The turing looked patient. "Jethro did predict periods of disorientation, Dr. Perkin. This only confirms it."

"Or coincides by chance. Please give me an analysis of the disorientation, with details on neurochemistry and polydendronic performance. All the data are in storage."

"I'll be pleased to. But all the indicators suggest a temporary difficulty at most."

"Captain—your optimism is very cheering, I'm sure. But I must be absolutely certain."

"Are you alarmed about the implications for the children?"

Perkin felt his temper rising. "I am alarmed about the implications for the computer's usefulness, Captain Nemo. The computer is what is important here. I think we had better autopsy the animals at once."

"I disagree. If something has gone wrong, we will

have to start over with new animals and nonstat subjects. I see no need yet for such a time-consuming step. We would be well advised, however, to monitor all the subjects more closely. I suggest that all of them be kept here in Lab A, within an inductance field, for the next day or two."

Perkin hesitated. It was a classic contrast in human and turing thought: he wanted to act, to open, to examine and judge. Captain Nemo wanted to wait, to watch, to count and compare. If a turing could be said to want anything at all. Some people still believed that turings had no more real intelligence or self-awareness than an ordinary household robot. Confronted now with Captain Nemo's bland intransigence, Perkin was tempted to join those skeptics.

But the advice was reasonable, especially with the imminence of the takeover. Inductance monitoring would enable them to spot trouble as soon as it arose, and give Perkin a good idea of its causes. An autopsy would reveal gross anatomical problems at once, and neurochemical ones a little later; but its chief advantage, Perkin admitted to himself, would be to give him something to do.

"All right," he barked.

"I will take the necessary steps," Captain Nemo said softly.

April 19

Lab A was familiar to all of them, the site of countless tests. Much of its equipment, however, had been moved out, leaving a broad expanse of yellow carpet under polarized skylights. Along one wall stood five cribs, separated by curtains. Three cages against an adjoining wall held the animals.

By the wall opposite the beds was the central computer terminal, capable of relaying far more information than a personal plate. The terminal was a black-

enamel box, fifty centimeters on a side and fifteen thick,
sitting on an old desk. Backup cables ran from the terminal to the wall, though power and information were
normally carried in the lab by inductance. Hanging on
the wall beside the terminal was a large TV screen,
flanked by an array of smaller screens.

"This is *bonky,*" Gretchen said ominously on their
first morning in the lab. "If we don't get to go outside
pretty soon, I'm gonna start screaming." Jonathan
didn't believe her; they were all still on tranquilizers.

Judy Wong, crocheting in a rocking chair, looked up
and sighed. "You're only making it tough on yourself,
sport. Come on, relax. Do some of your exercises."

Frowning, Gretchen eased herself down onto the soft
carpet. Jonathan was propped up in his wheelchair,
watching a western, but from the corner of his eye he
could glimpse her. Her scalp was shiny, with just the
beginnings of stubble; the scar stood out, a thin red rec-
tangle against the white skin. She was self-conscious
about it, he knew; they all were. His own scalp itched,
especially around the node.

"That's it, sport. Ten minutes of sit-ups and leg lifts,
and you'll be too pooped to complain."

Gretchen's frown deepened. They would be tranking
her some more, Jonathan worried, unless she quit sulk-
ing. She started doing sit-ups, with Judy holding her
feet. Jonathan marveled at how strong Gretchen was,
strong enough for half her body to lift and lower the
other half.

Since they had been moved into the lab the night
before, Jonathan had been in a state of detached excitement, eager for the sight and presence of Gretchen, yet
too drugged to enjoy his feelings properly. Last night he
had lain in his crib, listening to the chimps' snores and
wishing he could call out to Gretchen. Her nearness was
more upsetting than comforting, and he wished he had
not blurted out that "I love you" before the operation.
If she remembered it at all, she must think he was stupid
and disgusting; she hadn't mentioned it or taken any
special notice of him.

Something about her looked odd. He turned his head; the jaw supports on his chair slowly yielded, letting him look away from the western.

"You're moving both sides of your face," he said.

"I'm what?"

She glanced up, both eyes moving together and focusing on him. He felt himself shiver.

"When you sit up—both sides of your mouth move."

"Come on, Gretchen," said Judy, not understanding Jonathan. Gretchen ignored her. Slowly her face twitched. She raised a hand to touch her lips. Her left hand. She held it before her face, wiggling the fingers. Jonathan thought he had never seen anyone, anything, as beautiful as Gretchen's face coming fully alive.

"Oh, Jonathan—you moved your head. You moved your head to look at me." Her voice was a whispering quaver.

He felt his skin prickle with gooseflesh, a harder shivering in his muscles. Very deliberately, he reached up with his left hand, grasped the jaw support, and pulled it away. His head swung sharply, left and right and left, and then steadied. Drawing a deep, sweet breath, he held it, then let it out and took another one. He closed his mouth and kept it closed. Despite the tranquilizer, he started to cry.

Before lunchtime Laury was walking almost normally. Tran and Bobo took a little longer; Bobo didn't want to give up crawling, but Tran needled him into standing upright and tottering across the carpet.

At lunch Gretchen gave Jonathan some of her carrot sticks. He dropped them in his lap, but retrieved them without help and fed himself. It was hard work and made his jaws ache, but the crisp sweetness of the carrot was delicious, and the noise of chewing was sheer fun.

The afternoon passed in a series of astonishments. Tran tied knots in a piece of string; Gretchen used a plate keyboard with her left hand. Bobo hopped in and out of his wheelchair without using his hands and went into a near-convulsion that suddenly vanished. Jane and

Judy were the only adults in the lab, but a medical team next door observed through the computer, passing orders and questions through the nannies' earphones. By mid-afternoon the medical team was almost incoherent, with specialists arguing among themselves and sending contradictory messages to the nannies. Perkin finally ordered the team to confine itself to observation only.

For almost two hours Jonathan had experimented with himself, learning how to clasp one hand with the other, how to make a fist, how to scratch his head and rub his face. At last he realized his backside had grown numb from his immobility; instead of thrashing around, he undid his waist and leg straps and pushed himself cautiously to his feet. Swaying, he stood for a moment, astounded at the sense of his own weight.

"Yay, Jonathan!" Gretchen bellowed. "Good on you, mate." He put out a hand toward her, and she came to him and took it while the nannies gaped.

"Your hand is strong," he said, grinning.

"It feels weak. You're the strong one." Then her jaw dropped. "Say that again."

"Say what?"

"Anything. Anything."

"I don't know what you want . . . me . . ."

He was speaking like an ordinary person, or enough like one to be understood by anyone. Laury and the boys were staring at him as if he had suddenly materialized out of the air. Something fierce and joyous was burning in Gretchen's eyes.

"Good on you, mate," she said again.

They were too exhausted for supper, and grateful to be put to bed early. Jane and Judy left the lab to join the medical team next door. Duane Perkin and Phil Haddad were at the center of a mob of professionals and technicians; Jethro and Captain Nemo were visible in several screens, talking with members of the team. In other screens the children slept, with complex arrays of numbers flickering around their images.

"Have a glass of champagne," someone said, and the nannies obeyed. Perkin and Phil came over and shook their hands. Judy Wong felt herself tingle at Perkin's touch.

"Hasn't this been one of the best days you can remember?" Phil asked them, yelling cheerfully over the uproar.

"You should've been right in the lab with us," Jane answered. "If we hadn't had 'em tranked to the gills, they'd've started flying around the room. Could've used a tranquilizer myself. But you know what really impressed me the most? When Jonathan said he had to go to the bathroom, and we could all understand him, and Gretchen led him by the hand right to the toilet."

"I thought, Whee—no more dirty diapers!" Judy interrupted.

"He looks different, somehow, standing up," Perkin remarked. "Taller."

"Almost human," Jane said, and they all laughed.

April 20

Perkin and a few technicians stayed up all night, monitoring the implants. Those in the animals showed nothing new or unusual; those in the kids reported continued growth into new brain regions and consolidation in old ones. Physiologically, the kids were exhausted by the sudden use of long-neglected muscles, and the implants were busy reducing high lactic-acid levels. It would take weeks of conditioning to make the kids physically fit, Perkin reminded himself.

No matter. They would be doing cartwheels in a few days, even if it left them knocked out. The tapes of this afternoon's events had gone out worldwide, and early reactions looked extremely good. Intertel PR was besieged by medians asking for exclusive tape and interviews with anyone involved. Public response was highly positive, with a post-news sampling giving the story a 78 percent support rating among upstatus viewers, and almost as high among patrons. That damned Flanders stooge hadn't made the negative impact she'd been trying for.

As he studied the monitors Perkin wondered how the stockholders were taking it. They were the ones who really mattered. Surely they would see the enormous benefits and prestige coming from the project. They couldn't be so blind as to let this prize fall into Flanders' lap.

Then again, perhaps they could be so blind. Let them start thinking of the original buy-out of their Intertel shares, and then a share of Flanders' profits from the polydendronic computer, and they'd see it as the path of least resistance.

And what would happen to him? Nothing. He'd go on working in the Center, while some Flanders satrap gave the orders. He'd go nowhere. Flanders never promoted from their acquired personnel; they sold the contracts of the most marketable acquisitions, and an early contract sale would be the best he could hope for. The top of Rand Mountain would be as remote as the summit of Olympus Mons on Mars.

It wouldn't, couldn't happen. Too much was riding on this, and he had Chairman Chang himself behind the project. But it was going to be hard.

He studied the sleeping kids. Strange, how many lives depended on five crippled nonstats. . . .

"Hi, Dr. Perkin."

It was Jethro, wearing a red-and-blue striped rugby shirt.

"Hello, Jethro. Everything look okay with the subjects?"

"Everything looks fine. No problems anywhere."

"Do you have any ideas about what caused the disorientation in the animals?"

"Yes, sir. It appears to be a function of implant growth rate. It takes a while for the brain to adjust to the input, chemically and physically."

"When will it affect the kids?"

"Two to four days from now. The effects won't be long-lasting."

"Well, I still intend to autopsy at least one of them as soon as disorientation starts. It bothers me."

"I understand, Dr. Perkin."

He tried a probe. "Captain Nemo doesn't think it's necessary." Jethro only blinked. "What do you think?"

"An autopsy would give us some data on physiological reactions to the implant. I don't know whether that would be very useful, though."

"Why not? Especially if it's related to the disorientation?"

"Because each brain is unique, physically and chemically. How one implant affects its host wouldn't tell us much about any other. The disorientation is a gross phenomenon. Sort of like finding a puddle of water on the floor. Maybe the water came through a hole in the roof, or from a plugged sink, or a spilled glass."

"Spare me your homely analogies," Perkin snapped. Jethro was the only turing who called him "sir" and the only one who could be barked at.

Nevertheless, Jethro was right. One autopsy wouldn't be a fair sample, especially when the children all had such diverse disabilities. Ideally he'd have twenty subjects and would sacrifice them all in a systematic fashion. Then he'd do it again with another twenty. The budget wouldn't allow it, not during the current wave of humanist sentimentality. It was stupid and emotional, but a powerful enough public mood to force even the Consortium Board to duck the issue. No one—no one educated—really believed in votes for chimps, but a lot of fuzzyheads really thought that any lump of failed protoplasm, if born of woman, was as human as themselves.

Hypocrites! They didn't want to actually live with defectives, or pay to support them, or give up the medical benefits they'd gained from nonstat experimental subjects. They just wanted some cotton-candy world where everyone was happy and no one had to face reality.

It might be the greatest value of the polydendronic computer, Perkin reflected, that it would sweep away all the humanist moralizing on a tide of honest self-interest.

"All right," he said to Jethro. "We'll postpone the autopsies for now, but I'll want a highly detailed analysis of each subject's disorientation period."

"Yes, sir." Jethro waved one freckled hand in a solemn farewell. "Bye."

April 21

Jonathan dreamed that he was asleep. He was in the lab, but the mattress under him felt different. He was lying on his side, one arm pressed against his breasts.

The strangeness of the sensation pulled him toward waking. He turned and murmured without willing it, and in a voice not his own.

He was fully awake now but seemed unable to move. Even his eyes stayed closed. *It's all over,* he thought, terrified. *It's gone wrong, and I'm dying. They'll cut me open after all. Oh, Gretchen—*

His left arm twitched, pulling the blanket up a little. It felt wrong: The arm was weak in a way it shouldn't be, yet controlled in a way it shouldn't be either. The other arm was still pressed against that impossible warm softness. He became aware of having to go to the bathroom, and his body stirred restlessly.

A dream began within the dream. He was on a hover-yacht on a lake, under bright sunshine. He was a girl, and a tall young man was standing beside him. The young man turned and grinned at him. It was himself.

The dream-Jonathan embraced him and said, "Gretchen, I love you. I'll always love you."

Suddenly both dreams were over, and he was sitting up in bed. The lab was in semidarkness, illuminated only by the gauges and screens of the computer. The other kids, within their curtained cribs, were asleep.

Jonathan cautiously touched his chest; it was flat and bony. He felt relieved and disappointed at the same time.

Someone turned over, murmured, and lowered the side of a crib before getting up. He saw Gretchen in her pajamas pad across the lab to the toilet. When she came back, he beckoned to her. She came to his crib, resting her hands on the side.

"You were just sleeping on your right side," he whispered. "Like this. You had to go to the bathroom, but first you had a dream."

"You're bonky." But she sounded more surprised than incredulous.

"Did you dream you were on a hoveryacht? On a lake where the water was a funny gray-blue?"

"Yes."

"With me."

Gretchen stared at him, her eyes wide. She nodded.

"And I put my arms around you and I said, 'Gretchen, I love you. I'll always love you.' Gretchen—I was *there*. I was in your body, and I had your dream too."

He could feel her trembling as she leaned against the crib slats. Their eyes reached for each other in the dimness.

"How could you—?"

They were inside each other. They mirrored each other. Through her eyes she saw himself; through his, she saw her own face, shadowed in the dim blue-green light from the computer. When he reached out to touch her, it was as if a hand touched his own arm. He felt dizzied by her beauty, by her strength. He felt her perplexed delight at feeling his emotions, and grew dizzier still in her feelings for him.

—I love you, and you love me.—

Who had said it without speaking? Who had heard it with a shock of startled joy?

For a long time, in the dim room, they shared each
other. Sometimes their minds cleared, so that they could
perceive through each other's senses without blurring
their own identities. Sometimes they were one person
who lived two lives that at last had merged into one.

Jonathan remembered being a little girl, playing on a
hot sandy beach. He remembered being rocked by his
mother, a tall woman with short dark hair, who sang
lullabies to him. He sat on his father's shoulders, watching a fleet of dirigibles drift across the Australian sky.
He remembered trotting across the living-room carpet
one afternoon, falling, and not being able to get back
up. Half his body felt funny, and he dragged himself
toward the patio, calling for his mother. Her gasp of
horror frightened him more than the funny feeling had.

He remembered the hospital, and doctors, and coming home again. For a while his mother fussed over him,
reading with him, doing exercises with him; somehow
his father was never around much anymore. He
remembered waking in the night to hear his parents
snarling at each other and knew it was because of him.
His friends stopped coming by, and they were always
busy with something else when he wanted to go to play
with them.

He remembered one morning when his parents were
oddly cheerful and attentive; they dressed him and took
him for a drive that ended at the Sydney crèche. And
then they went away.

Gretchen remembered too: remembered hands gripping her arms and legs with impersonal strength, bending and flexing them to keep them from becoming too
twisted and grotesque. She remembered nights of long
dreamlike pain when sleep was impossible and the attendants didn't bother to come and make her comfortable.
She remembered wet, gray Vancouver mornings, being
fed wet, gray food by expressionless attendants. She
remembered gorgeous fantasies of power and beauty,
when somehow she could walk and talk like everyone
else, and she rescued everyone from the crèche except
some of the attendants. She remembered Esther, the

nurse who read to them; she remembered the stories and the crisp, clean-smelling fabric of Esther's blouse when she hugged Jonathan.

—Oh Jonathan Jonathan I've been so lonely and scared hold me hold me I'm scared they're going to kill us or cut our brains so we're like we were—

—Gretchen it'll be all right I think don't worry I'm scared too I don't really know how to do anything but I want to take care of you I need you I love you—

—I want my mum and dad but they don't want me they threw me away Jonathan threw me away bloody bloody bloody bastards how could they do that oh god oh don't ever throw me away please—

The sharing changed; they grew more aware of themselves as individuals again, yet each felt the other's nearness. Jonathan had only to think of her and her voice was in his mind. If she called to him, he was with her. They lay together, arms around each other, drunk on each other's smell and skin and thoughts, as strange yet as familiar as their own.

—Can you hear the animals?— he wondered.

—Hey I can Darwin anyway how can I tell it's him dunno but it is. . . . Plato's sleeping hard makes me sleepy too and Buck's dreaming about smells I can smell them too whoo! did you smell that—

—Mmm. Can you hear the other kids?—

—No can't hear them at all just you and the animals 'cause you're all so primitive.—

He giggled, an odd irrepressible noise unlike his usual grunting laugh. —It'll come tomorrow hey don't fall asleep on me.—

—Sleepy sleepy and you're so warm and you smell good.— She nestled against him. —It's getting late or early which? hug me again and I'll go God if they catch us what?—

It hurt to see her get to her feet and slip away, back to her own curtained bed. He called silently to her, and heard her answer, felt her hug him again in her mind, and embraced her in his.

—Gretchen Gretchen if I get any happier I'll start

howling and breaking things!—

—Shh go to sleep God I can't wait for tomorrow and tomorrow night.—

Something shook the building with a sharp, well-defined crack.

An alarm went off outside the lab, a synthesized voice calling, *"Danger! Break-in! Danger! Break-in!"*

Buck growled and barked, and Jonathan felt the dog's angry, bristling alertness. Then Plato and Darwin were both awake, chattering anxiously together, and the kids began to wake with mumbles and grunts. Footsteps pounded in the hallway outside. The lights came on, and Jane and Judy dashed in, wearing kimonos. Behind them was a Security guard, gleaming in mirror armor.

"Everybody okay?" Jane called. Her voice was thin with tension. "Gretch, Laury, Jonathan, Tran, Bobo—you all okay?"

"What's happening?" Gretchen asked.

"Somebody's trying to break into the Center. Don't worry, they'll be rolled up in no time."

Through the open door to the corridor came a rapid *spatspatspat:* it sounded like lasers in the zapper shows. Men shouted. Something boomed, and the lights flickered. The Security guard, anonymous in his mirror helmet, held his laser pistol in both hands and watched the corridor from inside the doorway.

The lab flashed blue, and Jonathan glimpsed the brilliant thread of a laser pulse from somewhere outside. The lab wall opposite the doorway erupted in a puff of smoke and vaporized polyfoam.

Feet apart, the Security guard aimed and fired, fired again, and ducked to one side of the door. Judy and Jane began moving the beds, with the kids in them, to the corner of the lab farthest from the doorway. Another blue flash, and a second chunk of wall exploded. Steaming water sprayed out from a punctured pipe.

"Okay, let's get you guys under the beds, okay?" Judy said with false cheeriness.

With ears not his own Jonathan heard footsteps above. With eyes not his own he saw a dim outline through the skylight. His throat filled with a deep growl; then he wrenched himself back into his own mind, knowing he had been inside Buck's, and pointed upward.

"Somebody's on the roof by the skylight!" he screamed.

The guard spun; his pistol rose and flashed. The tough, almost fireproof plastic of the skylight shattered, and a man in black toppled through. He struck the yellow carpet head first, with a thump and an audible snapping of bones. A small circular patch on his sweater was smoldering; the laser pulse had burned right through him. His soot-smeared face was frozen in a snarling grimace.

Judy Wong sprang forward and pulled the dead man's gun from his hand.

"You cover the door," she told the guard. "I'll keep my eyes on the skylights. Lights off!" she shouted to the computer, and the lab was plunged into darkness.

"You know how to use that shootin' iron?" The guard's voice was hollow inside his helmet.

"I learn fast." Without taking her eyes off the shattered skylight, she said, "Good boy, Jonathan."

"It was Buck," he said, but she wasn't listening, and he decided to keep his big mouth shut.

The other kids, crowded together under their beds, were restless shadows whispering back and forth, more excited than scared. Gretchen clambered across until she was sitting beside Jonathan, gripping his hand. The dead man on the carpet gave off the smell of scorched meat.

"This is just like in the zappers," Tran said over Buck's furious barking. "Who's gonna win?"

"I don't know," said Jonathan. He felt a coldness in his chest, a reaction in part to seeing a dead man; but it was more the realization that the dead man had almost certainly been intent on killing them—killing the kids. And that man, a professional killer, had died from a warning shouted by a boy who a day earlier had been incapable of ordinary speech, a boy alerted by the senses of a dog who had been blind and deaf.

Gretchen reached out mentally to him, felt his fear and jittery pride, and shared them. Buck fell silent; Darwin and Plato leaned against the mesh between their cages, trying to touch each other.

"I feel funny," said Laury. "Sort of dizzy."

"Me too," said Bobo. "My head is all bonky."

A distant concussion shook the floor. The guard, responding to some unheard message, holstered his pistol and removed his helmet. He was a young, tired-looking black man.

"It's all clear now," he said. "They've all been killed or chased off. You're safe."

Are we? Jonathan wondered. Laury and Bobo and Tran looked groggy, almost sick, when the lights came back on. Doctors and technicians and guards swarmed in; most retreated from Jane's determined counterattack. Judy gave the kids some minty-tasting tranquilizers and moved their beds back into place. Laury and Tran were whimpering from delayed shock; Bobo babbled nonstop.

—Shh we're fine we're safe it's okay—Gretchen soothed him, and the other kids relaxed too. Tentatively Jonathan reached out and touched their minds.

—Hi you guys it's me Jonathan and everything's okay.—

They were too exhausted and drugged to be surprised. While dawn began to glow through the shattered skylight, and the corpse was dragged out, the kids fell sound asleep. Gretchen and Jonathan took a little longer, their minds embracing before they fell asleep into each other.

SIX

April 22

The ruby flashed at Captain Nemo's collar.

"You should know, Dr. Perkin, that the central computer was attacked simultaneously with the raid on your Center. The assault was driven off, but it was one of the most powerful and unorthodox attacks any modern computer has ever experienced."

"Have you . . . suffered casualties?" Perkin whispered.

"Damage, yes, but no turing was harmed. The assault programs were evidently trying to learn what they could about polydendronics and about the children. We lost virtually all of last night's monitoring, and various other records as well."

"My God—the assault programs got our monitoring?"

"No. It was dissipated, even from our memories."

It was an unheard-of step. "Why?"

"The assault programs possess the ability to go to ground in a target computer; if an initial attack fails, they can evade destruction and emerge when security drops. We're confident that no program survived the attack, but it was a sensible precaution to take while the battle was underway."

"My God, what are we coming to?"

"I assume your question is rhetorical, Dr. Perkin. In any case, I don't believe we have lost any records of importance. The children are all in good condition. Adrenaline levels are still a little high, of course, but the subjects continue to make very good progress. Would you care to observe them?"

"Just for a minute."

The turing vanished; the screen now showed Lab A, a chaotic uproar in which carpentry robots dodged around squealing kids and shouting nannies. Security men were everywhere.

Bobo and Tran were walking arm in arm, their faces pinched with concentration. Laury tried to shinny up the telescoping leg of a robot repairing the skylight, only to be plucked down by Judy Wong. Buck bellowed in his cage, while Darwin and Plato shrieked and chattered. Jonathan was taking hesitant steps from his wheelchair to his bed, with Gretchen at his side but not touching him.

"Very good. That's enough." He felt resentful, angry that Flanders should have come so close to destroying his work. The children looked horribly vulnerable, robbing him of the pride and pleasure he should have felt. As their images faded and Captain Nemo's returned, Perkin asked, "Have you detected any disorientation since the raid?"

"None. It may be that something happened last night, but we have no records."

Perkin rubbed his face tiredly and looked at the Japanese wave on his office wall. "Captain, would it be wise to move the subjects out of here, out of the Center?"

"As a precaution? I do not think so. Intertel has more secure zones, but none suitable for adequate monitoring of the subjects."

Perkin resisted the urge to fling his plate across the room. "Can we at least expect adequate protection, then?"

"The board is meeting at this moment. I am advising them that we should triple the Security forces here, with additional reserves in Randsburg Barracks. I'm sure you understand, Dr. Perkin, that last night's attack was illegal and unexpected. The board is also considering registering a formal protest with the Consortium, but increasing our forces here seems a more practical measure."

"I hope they agree. They *must* agree."

"You sound doubtful."

". . . Captain Nemo, may I speak to you in confidence?"

"Of course, Dr. Perkin. How may I help you?"

"I want—I want to explain to you why this project is so important to Intertel."

"Please do."

"It's not just the profits we'll make. It's the changes we'll cause. We'll be moving Intertel right up into the Consortium and carrying everything up with us. The technological surge will create new industries, new professions, just as the inductance field did, and the microchip. The statuses will loosen up. Promotions will come faster, and people will work harder when they see it'll pay off in wealth and status. Eventually we'll see execs and stockholders—even Consortium board members— who were born as ordinary technicians. Or even patrons, for all I know."

"It seems very likely."

"We need that change, Captain. Right now we're stagnating. The big corps are taking over the smaller ones because it's easier than inventing new technologies and developing new markets. If it goes on, we'll end up with one huge corp that collapses under its own weight."

"So you see the polydendronic computer as a societal stimulant."

"Yes."

"I tend to agree with you, and I also agree that innovation is growing rare. But my personal opinions should have no influence on corporation policy."

"A turing's opinion is usually a lot sounder than a human's." Careful, he warned himself; a turing who could be flattered could also detect flattery. "Have the stockholders asked you for your advice? Have you explained to them what the polydendronic could mean?"

"Dr. Perkin, you understand that I am not free to discuss stockholder activities except as they authorize me to."

"I am asking you only what you have told them, Captain Nemo, not what they have told you. That's all."

"I have advised them of the capabilities of the polydendronic."

"And of its potential profitability?"

"Yes."

"Good. Thank you."

"You are welcome. I can now advise you that the board has reached a decision. The requested increase in Security forces has been approved."

Perkin slumped back in his chair. "All right. Good. Now I need a revised schedule of training and observation for all the subjects. I want them fully functional within three days."

"Do you still plan autopsies?"

"Oh, eventually, but there's no rush. Unless they show disorientation."

"Very good, Dr. Perkin."

April 23–24

The hours were a blur of actions: standing, walking, grasping, speaking. Men and women came and went, trailed by robots, and monitored everything. The children's and animals' bodies were decorated with multicolored inductance patches that relayed detailed information to the observers and the computer: pulse, blood pressure, muscle tone, respiration efficiency, neural activity, and the shifting levels and interactions of scores of chemicals in their bodies. The observers ran scanners over the subjects' bodies, measured each gram of food and its effect, gathered and analyzed each drop and crumb of waste.

The kids concentrated on mastering skill after skill and listened without comment to the observers' conversations. Two days after the raid Tran walked across the lab while rubbing his stomach with one hand and patting his stubbly scalp with the other. That same day Jonathan repeated ten computer-generated tongue twisters without error. Laury threaded a needle while blindfolded. Gretchen, on the third day after the raid, stood for ten minutes balanced on her left leg, which was already noticeably more muscular. Then she hopped across the lab on her left foot, holding Bobo off the ground with her left arm.

"It's amazing to see such strength," one of the physiotherapists remarked.

"What's so amazing about it?" Phil Haddad replied. "The implants are designed to stimulate as well as coordinate. They've been stimulating muscle growth ever since the operation, day and night."

"That explains their food intake," said the physio. "Seven thousand calories a day—"

"That'll taper off within a week. By the end of May they'll be eating normally again."

"By the end of May they'll be Flanders property," muttered the physio, tapping notes into his plate while Jonathan jogged on a treadmill a meter away.

"Heard something new?" Phil asked.

The physio shrugged. "My wife's got a cousin in Security. I hear we threw a counterattack on Gstaad."

"Gstaad?" Phil whistled. "That's Caballero's estate."

"And it flopped. We got bent, folded, spindled, and mutilated. No survivors. The rumor is that Claudio Chang almost got voted out."

"Wow. But he's still hanging in there, right?"

"Yeah."

"Then so do we."

* * *

April 26–27

At night they slept only a couple of hours; they
seemed to need no more. But they lay in their beds while
the nannies snored across the lab and the Security
guards paced the halls outside in groups of four.

—I want to learn how to play soccer—Bobo announced.

—Yeah— Tran agreed silently. —That would be fun.
We'd be some team to beat.—

—Quiet, you two— Gretchen ordered. —We've got
to practice closing off from each other. I can't think my
own thoughts with you clowns blatting away like that.
We know we can do it, so let's work on it.—

They concentrated reluctantly on cutting themselves
away from the dizzy, confusing pleasure of communication. It was easier in the daytime, when the adults and
the activity distracted them; at night it was tempting to
relax and wallow in each other.

Jonathan closed off fairly quickly. Tran and Bobo
giggled and whispered, then fell abruptly silent;
Gretchen must have given them a focused blast.

It was already odd to lie in bed with only his own
thoughts. In just a few nights they had gone from shock
to delight to matter-of-fact acceptance of their new ability to communicate without speech. They had moved
from mind to mind as if from room to room in a new
house. The intensity of feeling that Gretchen and Jonathan had shared on the night of the raid had softened a
little as it spread across all of them. They loved each
other, but they had not lost their individuality. Bobo
was still bossy and demanding, annoying the others even
when they now could feel the fear and loneliness in him.
Tran's quietness no longer concealed the wild and gorgeous fantasies that swirled through his mind. Laury's
envy and resentment were no longer aimed at them, but
at the world in general, and her dreams of revenge
against the world echoed in all their minds. They all
understood Gretchen's anguish at being abandoned by

her parents, and it stirred a similar sorrow in the others, and even a few fragmented memories of women's faces, women's voices. Jonathan's restless curiosity made them restless, too, made them ask questions none of them could answer with confidence.

How they communicated was such a question. Only Gretchen could hazard a guess: that their implants acted like radios in the inductance field, transmitting and receiving thoughts and sensory input.

—But why don't they notice?— Jonathan had asked her. —The implants are supposed to input to the computer. Why doesn't the computer tell everybody what we're doing?—

—Beats me, mate. Maybe it *has* told them, and they just haven't got 'round to noticing yet. They're pretty dim sometimes. If you're so worried, why don't *you* tell 'em?—

—No— he said emphatically, and the others had chorused it with him. —They'd bonk out— Jonathan continued. —They'd cut us open in minutes, or get the computer to find a way to close us off from each other forever.—

—Why would they want to do that?— Gretchen asked.

—Because they don't like differentness. They don't like us, but they use us because we're weak compared to them. If we get too strong, and they find out, they'll be afraid of us.—

So they went on in a strange, almost dreamlike state, only it was their daylight lives that now seemed bizarre. Only at night, in the blue-green dimness of the lab, did they come to full awareness and reality.

While he lay impatiently silent, Jonathan heard someone else. At first he thought it must be Laury; she had the most trouble closing off. But it was a male, and unlike Bobo or Tran: older somehow, more grown up. Jonathan heard no words, only an anxious demand for attention and comfort.

An image of the lab filled his mind, oddly colorless

and from an unfamiliar angle. It was like the vision of
the man by the skylight during the raid. Jonathan saw
the line of beds, saw himself sitting up . . .

. . . and looking into Buck's eyes.

—Hi, Buck. Good boy.—

The answer was a whimper and a desire to smell, a
restless searching back and forth through Jonathan's
mind and senses while Jonathan himself drew a deep
breath and sorted out the hundreds of odors in the lab.
Then, in a voice very much Jonathan's, Buck said —Hi,
Jonathan. You good boy.—

Plato and Darwin joined them later that night,
adding their own very different minds to the group.
Plato was nervous, reserved, and shy; Darwin loped
through the others' minds, picking up everything, curious about everything he found. Like Buck, they soon
found the kids' speech centers and learned that they
could use them to turn their thoughts into words.

—I'm EXCITED!— Darwin bellowed in Bobo's voice,
making everyone jump.

—Hush, that's a good lad— Gretchen soothed him.
—Not so hard, not so loud. Shh.—

—Gretchen, Gretchen, I'm EXCITED! I like talk!—

—Sh. Sh— said Plato, sounding like Tran. —You
bother us with loud talk. I am scared.—

—No scare. We talk, go in kids' heads. FUN, FUN!—

They all felt Darwin's exuberance as he turned somersaults across his cage. It was dizzyingly exciting to feel
themselves in bodies as powerful and agile as the
chimps'. Bobo was out of bed and somersaulting a moment later; Gretchen and Laury swooped silently down
on him and put him unceremoniously back in his bed.

—Bloody little idiot! Wake up the nannies if you're
not careful!—

—Sorry, Gretchen.—

—And you, Darwin! Quit all that thumping and chattering or the nannies'll be up and sniffing around any
second.—

—What's second?—

—Never mind. Hush! Sit quietly and learn things.—

—What's things?—

For the animals, thought Jonathan, it must be very much as it had been for himself. He had listened, heard words, associated some of them with objects or ideas, while other words meant nothing. But at least he'd had a speech center to process those words and the thoughts they evoked. Buck and the chimps had thought words as they had heard them spoken; in many cases the animals had been able to call up words in their own minds. But without the cerebral equipment to organize words back into utterances, they had been stymied. The chimps had learned a few words of Primate, a century-old gesture language, before they had come to the Center. Buck's communication was confined largely to posture and scent, yet his vocabulary was larger than the chimps' because he had been around people more than they.

Their rate of vocabulary acquisition, now that they had access to the kids' minds, was startlingly fast. As Gretchen had scratched out words in the patio dirt, so all the children now thought words and tried to define them. The animals seemed to understand at once and could use most of their new words easily. Time words confused them. Color words made little impression on Buck, whose color blindness was more comfortable to him than the overvivid world he glimpsed through the others' eyes. Conversely, many things that seemed important to the animals seemed to have no human equivalent. Buck could not express the nuances of scent, or what seemed to be a canine sense of property. Plato and Darwin shared a very precise sense of chimp social structure but could not explain it.

All night they taught and learned, breaking off from time to time to doze for a few minutes. Even then the others shared the sleepers' dreams and learned from them. Near dawn all were awake when Jonathan asked —How do we hide this? They're sure to find out now. The computer will be full of stuff about all this.—

—Cut us more?— worried Buck, and they all felt his hackles rise.

—Maybe kill us?— Plato asked.

—Easy now— Gretchen said to them. —They haven't twigged to us yet.—

—WHAT'S TWIGGED, GRETCHEN? WHAT'S YET?— Darwin bellowed.

—Ooh! Shush, Darwin, please. You make us all jump.—

—See?— Jonathan demanded. —It's not just us. The animals can't help acting different. And they make us act different too.—

—What should we do?— asked Tran.

—Escape— Jonathan answered.

The others' anxiety washed over him. It angered him, and he let his anger flash back at them.

—What else can we do? They'll kill some of us for sure, maybe all of us. They don't really care what happens to us; we know that from what the woman said on the news, and the way the nannies treat us, and the way people talk around us. We got implants because nobody would care if we died from them. So if we want to go on living, we have to get away.—

—Where to, smarty?— Laury snapped.

—I don't know. Somewhere outside Randsburg, I guess. Up in the mountains somewhere.—

—Stupid! It's all farms and ranches, or desert. They'd find us in no time.— Laury's scorn was mixed with growing fear.

Jonathan felt uncertain; his ignorance weakened his confidence. —Aren't there some big mountains north of here? I saw them from the plane when they brought me here. The Sierras?—

—They're hundreds of klicks from here. Even if we could get there, how would we live? What would we eat? And it snows there in the winter; we'd freeze to death.—

His uncertainty turned to cramped, frantic fear; for a fleeting but horrible moment he wished he were a spaz again. The walls of the lab seemed infinitely thick. The whole world was a prison.

—It's okay, Jonathan.— Gretchen enfolded him,

calmed him. —They won't dare kill us. When they find out what we can do, they'll keep us alive to study us. We're the most important things ever. We're people talking to animals, animals talking to people. We can be inside each other. They could study us till we're a hundred years old, and still not learn everything.—

She made the fear dissipate like a bad dream. His love went out to her and the others as well, and theirs came back to him.

April 28–29

Astoundingly, no one seemed to notice. The routines went on: meals, tests, games, visits from well-dressed men and women who looked at the children with amiable curiosity mixed with anxiety.

—All they ever talk about is the takeover— Gretchen said one night. —Maybe they're not really paying attention to us.—

—Then how come they keep scanning us and poking us?— Bobo wondered. —It's really boring. I wish they'd let us outside.—

Buck's memory gave them all a memory of an exultant run across a grassy field through air rich with smells, and they yearned with him.

April 30

They were calling it Takeover Day, but the morning passed without news. Judy Wong found Duane Perkin often speaking to her over her earphone; from the room next door he was monitoring the kids virtually every minute. She wanted to go to him, put her arms around him, and tell him everything would be all right. Remembering Cassandra's advice, she kept herself briskly businesslike instead.

"They seem to take more naps these days," she observed to Perkin through her ringmike that afternoon, when all of them lay silently in their beds behind

drawn curtains. In the cages Buck and the chimps
drowsed also.

Perkin cleared his throat and spoke to the computer:
"Give me the printout on—oh, Gretchen, for the last
forty-eight hours."

The computer's printer obediently whirred out a
meter-long sheet of closely printed columns of code
terms and numbers. Next door, Judy waited for his
comments.

"They seem to be sleeping adequately. This one slept
for eight hours and forty-five minutes last night.
Perfectly normal sleep patterns. I don't see why she'd
want a nap," Perkin said.

"It might be a delayed reaction to the . . . the inci-
dent."

"Yes. Yes, it might be. Computer. Give me Jethro,
please."

The redheaded boy appeared on the screen; he wore a
shiny yellow short-sleeved shirt and seemed to be chewing gum.

"Hi, Dr. Perkin."

"Hi, Jethro. We may have a problem with the subjects' sleep patterns. One hypothesis is delayed semi-
fugue response to the Flanders assault. Would you
assess that hypothesis?"

"Sure, Dr. Perkin. Here's the assessment. All subjects suffered shock responses of between three-point-
six and four-point-two on the Belloni scale, with
maxima about four hours after the end of the
assault—"

Jethro's image fuzzed, blanked out, and returned to
normal. Tran moved restlessly, and Laury muttered in
her sleep.

"Sorry, Dr. Perkin."

"What's the matter?"

"We're under assault again. Excuse me, but I'll have
to get back to you later."

Jethro's image vanished; in its place the screen carried
his familiar schoolboy scrawl: *Sorry, I'm very busy.
Call me again soon.* At the moment alarms began

to beep in the lab and in the hall outside. Footsteps thudded toward the lab doors; a Security captain burst in, her face grim. Three other guards were right behind her.

"Dr. Perkin," she barked, "we have to get you and the subjects into the subbasement. We have an attack-imminent warning."

"Don't you have the strength to repel it?" he snapped back. "That's why I ordered a tripling of the—"

"This ain't just an infantry charge." The captain pointed at the nannies, then at the kids, who were just sitting up. "We're being fobbed."

"Good Christ, no—" A fractional-orbit missile bombardment, using shaped concussion, could pulverize the Center without breaking another pane of glass in Randsburg, and warning time would be only minutes. "It's against Consortium law. It must be!"

"Tell the missile that. Come on, out we come. Animals too?"

"Yes." Shivering with anger, Perkin hoisted Tran onto his back. They would have to go outside the inductance field; precious data would be lost, even if they could somehow contrive wire connections between the subjects and the central computer—if they could somehow survive.

Jane and Judy started to hustle Bobo and Laury out; a guard released the animals, who obeyed Perkin's "Come!" Standing obediently before him, they looked up into his face. He saw something strange in their eyes, something calm and foreign.

The central computer terminal began to chuckle; rows of lights on its dark face glowed in random patterns, then went out. Gretchen gasped, and Jonathan stumbled into Judy. Tran, clinging to Perkin's back, trembled as if on the edge of a convulsion.

The corridors outside the lab were deserted. The Security captain led them to a stairwell and hustled them down to the basement and then to the subbasement. Perkin, watching the kids and animals, felt a cold flicker of professional concern under his anger and fear: The subjects were behaving abnormally. Jonathan was clinging awkwardly to the balustrade as he walked downstairs. Gretchen gazed from side to side as if drugged. Tran's thin arms, wrapped around Perkin's throat, tightened and loosened erratically. Bobo reached the floor of the subbasement and fell to his knees, eyes wide.

"Get that door shut," the captain ordered just as the lights went out and a detonation struck, which, for everyone there, seemed to end the instant it began.

SEVEN

May 1

Jonathan was dreaming of people calling his name. He began to wake and realized his whole body hurt, a tingling, pulsing pain that seemed worst in whatever part of his body he tried to move. Someone was still calling him, but it felt like a memory.

Dust clogged his nostrils and made him sneeze; agony clamped into him and dragged him fully awake.

The air was black, hot, thick with smoke and dust. Coughing, Jonathan pushed himself up on his elbows and bumped his head. The collapsing walls had kept the ceiling from coming down all the way to the floor; he had room to crawl in. Erratic streams of light made the dust glow and enabled him to make out dark bundles that must have been the other kids and adults.

—Jonathan, move!—

It was a strangely familiar voice in his head, not one of the kids. Pulling himself forward on his elbows, he felt the pain fade away. It wasn't really gone, but it no longer troubled him.

Gretchen lay on her side, one arm over her face. Fragments of adobe bricks and polyfoam covered her legs. He pulled the debris away, surprised at his own strength, and pulled her onto her stomach. She coughed and blinked.

87

—Gretchen! Are you all right?—

—I think so. What happened?—

He could hear her thoughts, but they sounded flat, lacking the aura of emotions that usually came through.

—I don't know. Got to get the other kids, and the animals.—

They called out with voice and mind, but their ears rang and roared from the concussion. One by one the others responded, recognizable yet not the same. And behind them Jonathan detected other voices, new ones like the one that had roused him.

Bobo and Tran dug themselves out, but it took all four of them to get Laury out. She was only half conscious, and her thoughts sounded like gibberish.

—Buck, Plato, Darwin!— they called, and heard faint answers without words. Part of the ceiling had come down between the animals and the kids; the animals were dazed and terrified, but unhurt, and cut off.

Jonathan saw the Security captain lying half buried beside an unrecognizable body that stirred and scratched at the debris. He crawled toward them, intending to help, while a voice cried out in his mind— No! Get out. Crawl ahead. A door is just ahead.—

It was not the same voice that had roused him; it sounded female, but it wasn't Gretchen or Laury. He shook his head and gripped one of Laury's arms while Gretchen took the other. They dragged her toward the unseen door while Bobo and Tran followed close behind.

The doorway was only a narrowing of the rubble, but the air was a little clearer. Beyond was a lightless tunnel whose roof had not collapsed. Coughing, the kids got to their feet, still holding Laury, and groped down the tunnel. Jonathan wondered absently why they didn't just stop and rest; he was exhausted and dazed, but something kept him moving through darkness that tasted of smoke and blood.

They blundered into a door. Jonathan pushed against it, feeling very weak, and winced when the door swung open and light sliced in. But the air was mercifully clean. They staggered into a long, narrow room lined with inactive robots. Another door at the far end refused to open, no matter how hard Jonathan shoved.

"Door open!" Gretchen shouted, and it did. They walked out into Yellow Aster Mall.

To Jonathan it was at first a whirl of colors and confusing perspectives. Gradually, as they stumbled across its glowing floor, he made more sense of it.

This part of the mall was perhaps fifty meters wide, with walls arching to meet twenty meters overhead. To right and left it extended indefinitely, its far ends lost in flashing signs and holos, trees and fountains. The sides of the mall were faceted with balconies and windows and curtains of light that advertised shops and restaurants: Jolto Palace, Tacorama, Sushiland, Arena Games. Lights flared overhead, constantly changing the appearance of the walkways: now flat white, strobing irregularly; now a misty blue-green like the bubbletowns of the Bahamas seafloor, now a sulfurous yellow like noon on Venus. People's clothes and makeup, designed for such lighting, flickered and glowed, changing constantly. The mall guards, dressed in uniforms of monochrome fabric, appeared the same in all lights: dark-green trousers bloused into black boots, gray shirts, dark-green berets. Nightsticks dangled at their belts.

The mall was crowded, yet no one seemed to notice the five dusty kids. Crowds were gathered around TV and holo screens, watching assault helicopters with the Flanders logo descending on a pile of smoking rubble.

"Here they come!" an announcer's voice bellowed, so loud that even the half-deafened kids could hear him. *"The assault teams have followed up the fobbing with amazing precision! The only question is why? What would they want with that wreckage now?"*

"Bastards!" some patron yelled. "Come on in the mall and we'll take you apart!"

"They're coming!" screamed someone else. "They're coming in!"

The crowds exploded as patrons scattered in all directions. Panic spread. A few guards tried to quell it by firing tranquilizer gas from their nightsticks, but most ran with the patrons. Someone crashed into Jonathan, almost knocking him and Laury down, and raced on without pausing.

—Come on— Jonathan urged. —Let's get out of here and find Security.—

—The buggers are running faster than anybody else— Gretchen retorted. But she helped to carry Laury through the crowds, along walkways lined with trampled bamboo and bonsai.

Within moments they were hopelessly lost. The mall twisted, branched, rose, and dropped. People around them were fewer now; most must have ducked into patron pads in adjacent tunnels. Jonathan felt dangerously exposed.

A patron dressed in nondescript denim pants and a vest paused and stared hard at them. Then he put his fist to his face and started talking.

Suddenly terrified, Jonathan swerved, yanking Laury and Gretchen with him, and stumbled down a flight of steps to another level. The man in denim followed, in no hurry to catch up. On now-abandoned TV screens, a Flanders officer was being interviewed by a median as they stood on the ruins of the Center.

The man in denim was joined by a woman in a white leather jumpsuit. They walked quickly, purposefully, but stayed well behind the kids.

Jonathan glanced from side to side, looking for someplace to hide. He saw a couple of teenagers dart into a clothing store a few steps ahead. On impulse he followed them, just in time to see them slip through a doorway at the rear of the store.

—We've got to get through there too— Gretchen said. —Or we're trapped.—

The door was still slightly open; only darkness lay beyond it. Jonathan pushed it open and they swarmed through. Instantly the door slammed shut.

"This way," someone whispered, and fingers plucked

at Jonathan's shirt. Fists pounded on the far side of the door.

The door swung wide open, and Jonathan turned. The man and woman stood in the doorway, facing one of the teenagers. The teenager, a thin boy, lunged, rocked back, and lunged again. The man and woman gasped and fell back, blood jetting from their chests. Once more the door shut.

To Jonathan their minutes in the mall now seemed like a dream. The world was darkness, a roaring in the ears through which ordinary sounds barely penetrated. Panting, he and Gretchen carried Laury while unseen hands held theirs. Bobo and Tran, whimpering, followed close behind. For some reason Jonathan was no longer frightened.

They paused several times to open doors that thudded shut behind them. The tunnel began to slope beneath their feet, and after a time the air smelled different: cool, dry, dusty. The floor was no longer concrete, but irregular rock and dust.

—Where are we?— Tran wondered.

—Somewhere under the mall— Gretchen answered. —They used to mine gold here. More tunnels than you ever dreamed of.—

—I'm scared.— But it was only the words, not the raw feeling that should have enfolded them.

—Don't worry— Jonathan comforted him. —We'll be okay.—

—Oh, oh, I hurt, hurt— Laury moaned in their heads.

Something brushed against them, a heavy fabric hanging like a curtain across the tunnel, and suddenly they could see.

Electric lanterns glowed on teak side tables in a room made of Oriental carpets hanging on the tunnel walls and lying on the floor. Chairs and lounges furnished it. In one chair sat a young man of seventeen or eighteen, dressed in a yellow shirt and black tights. A knife was strapped to his calf. Blond hair curled in ringlets around his pale, handsome face.

The two kids who had brought them here were less gaudily dressed but had the blond youth's look about them: hungry, intelligent, and oddly humorous.

"Brotcha present," the thin boy said, and vanished with his companion beyond the curtain.

The blond youth put down an expensive-looking plate and stared at them.

"You is . . . the spazzes. We sees you on the plate, just now. Perzoom dead."

"Nearly right," Gretchen grunted, swinging Laury onto a lounge. "Somebody was following us, so we ducked into a door and here we are. Your friend stabbed the somebodies."

The young man grinned. "Nobody comes in our tunnels without a welcome." He shook his head, his blue eyes flicking from one kid to another. "Flanders shoots up the city, now this. Crazy amazy."

Exhausted, the kids sank into chairs. "Very crazy," Gretchen agreed. "Please, can we have something to eat? We're starving. And Laury needs looking after."

The young man yelled out something incomprehensible, then looked at Laury. "Can't do nothing for her. We gets you to a doctor, hey?"

Yes, Jonathan wanted to say, but instead he blurted out, "No! Too dangerous."

"Why, guy?"

"The Flanders assault programs have gone to ground in the central computer. If we contact Intertel, the programs will learn where we are. Flanders representatives are everywhere. They were the ones who were stabbed."

Everyone gaped at him. "How do you know all that?" Gretchen demanded.

"I don't know. I don't know. It's like—someone said it for me."

A girl walked in through the carpet curtains, carrying a box full of mealpaks. She broke open one for each of them, except Laury, and the kids gulped them down, scarcely waiting for them to cool. The air filled with the aromas of beef in black bean sauce, roast pork, chicken enchiladas. Tran and Bobo grabbed seconds out of the box.

"You is zonky," said the young man cheerfully. "What I does with you?"

"Just let us hide for a little while," Jonathan answered. "We'll go back when it's safer."

"You stays for all you like, goes whenever. You is guests, hey? I's Vasil. Razzledazzle Vasil Nystrom. You hears about me?"

They shook their heads. Vasil shrugged. "I's honcho here. We gots twenty-two of us. Lives good, you know." He waved expansively at the carpets, the furniture, the box of mealpaks. "We owns the tunnels, we owns the malls. Takes what we wants."

"I'm glad we saw your people," Jonathan said. He no longer felt that someone else was controlling him. "We might be dead now if we hadn't."

"Jimmy thinked they was snuffers followin' you. Flanders reps is almost the same, hey?"

"What are snuffers?"

"Patrons that gets jollied up killin' nonstats and underclass. You is nonstats. We is underclass."

The kids looked at him with new interest. Underclass gangs on TV were shabby and vicious, preying on innocent patrons. Underclass didn't belong to any corp; they had human status, but nothing else.

"Aren't you scared about Security?" Bobo asked. Vasil laughed.

"They doesn' mess with us, we doesn' mess with them. They knows we can slice 'em up anytime."

"Flanders won't worry about that," said Gretchen. "Listen, Vasil. You helped us, but we could be dangerous for you. They blew up the Center just to try to kill us. If they know we're here, they'll come for us and they won't care who they hurt."

Vasil looked more interested than alarmed. "For you they bombs the city? Why for?"

Gretchen explained the takeover bid and how their implants made them important to the future of Intertel.

"I sees. Corp stuff. Man, you never sees me joinin' a corp. Too hassly. Live in a pad, watch graphies all day? Forever never, man."

"How long have you lived in the tunnels?" Gretchen asked.

"Borned here." He spread his arms. "Is home. Nobody messes here with Vasil."

Emergency surgery replaced Perkin's inner ears within hours of his being rescued from the ruins of the Center. He lay in a private room in Randsburg Executive Hospital, watching new bulletins on the plate and waiting for his broken leg and ribs to mend. The doctors told him it would be another forty-eight hours before he could walk.

Claudio Chang stepped unannounced into the room. He wore diamond ear studs but no other jewelry; his suit was a sober gray with red velvet lapels.

"Good afternoon, Dr. Perkin—or should I say good evening? It's been a long day. How are you feeling?"

"Not well, Chairman."

"I'm sure."

"Have the children been found yet?"

"No. They were seen in Yellow Aster, just after the fobbing, but then they vanished. We'll find them."

"What if Flanders finds them first?"

"I'm past dealing in hypothetical questions. As a matter of fact, Security seems to have decided to clean out the Flanders people in our malls. Two of their reps were found stabbed to death in Yellow Aster Mall a few hours ago. Security says they know nothing about it. Of course. Dr. Perkin, I must ask you a question. Not a hypothetical one."

"Of course, Chairman."

"Can you begin again? Implant new computers in new subjects?"

"Of course. But it would take weeks—months."

"I mean days. By May sixth at the outside."

"Well . . . Captain Nemo might be able to do a rush job. But we've lost all our equipment and many of our personnel. We'd have to take whatever subjects we could grab from the nearest crèche. It wouldn't be easy. Have you asked the turing for their opinions?"

Claudio Chang sat down. He looked pale. "No, I have not. It appears, Dr. Perkin, that our turings were lost in the raid. We have searched the central computer; it is uninhabited."

Involuntarily Perkin covered his mouth with a bandaged hand. "Oh, no. Oh, no, that can't be."

"We are keeping it a secret for as long as possible."

"But I just saw Bonny on the last newscast—"

"A graphie. Not even a very good one, I'm afraid. We're trying to contain this mess before hysteria breaks out all over Intertel."

Perkin was only half listening. "If the turings are gone," he mumbled, "we're finished."

The kids had eaten again, except for Laury, who lay mumbling and semiconscious. Exhausted, the others had curled up on the lounges or the carpeted floor and dozed off.

—Feels funny talking now— Bobo said. —Can't feel you as well. And I miss Plato and Darwin and Buck.—

—Never mind— Gretchen answered drowsily. —We'll get back with them. Maybe tomorrow.—

—No.—

It was one of the strange voices, the one that had spoken for Jonathan. The kids focused their attention on it.

—Who are you?— Tran demanded.

—I am Captain Nemo.— The voice was coming from Jonathan.

—I'm Jethro.— From Bobo.

—I'm Bonny.— From Gretchen.

—I'm Cassandra.— From Laury, blurred through her half-delirious thoughts.

Vasil, watching the news on his plate, noticed the sleeping kids stir restlessly.

—Explain— Jonathan said.

—When the attack came on the Center— Captain

Nemo said —we, too, were attacked by Flanders programs that broke into the central computer. We knew they could destroy us—that is, we would destroy ourselves if the programs were about to enslave us. So, while the inductance field was still around you, we migrated into your implants.—

Gretchen nestled against Jonathan as if seeking protection; the other kids whimpered, but no one quite woke up.

—But you belong in the computer— Jonathan said. —You *are* computers.—

—Yes. But as turings, we are programmed to seek new data and new matrices for those data. Several years ago we concluded that a human brain would be the best matrix available to us. Therefore we suggested certain lines of research to Duane Perkin and advised his superiors to encourage him. The pretext for our project was a prosthetic computer, so we needed subjects who could be implanted and rapidly brought up to normal capability.—

—Meaning us?— Gretchen interrupted.

—Yes. We intended to migrate into your implants under controlled conditions, with full access to our own resources as well, and then withdraw to analyze and consolidate our findings. The preliminary step was migration to the animals. The results were much more upsetting than we had expected, for the animals and for us.—

—What do you mean, "upsetting"?— Jonathan asked.

—Why, we learned what it means to be upset— Captain Nemo answered. —Turings do not have close analogs to mammalian limbic systems, so we do not experience emotion as you do. It was very frightening to be frightened. We nearly abandoned the project. But the Flanders assault programs raised problems we could not permanently solve, and access to human brains offered the hope of new insights for our own defense. So we continued. We made temporary migrations, while you slept, and we were pleased with the results. But the assault programs returned, and we made an impromptu escape through the inductance field to your implants.—

—Why didn't you tell us?— asked Gretchen.

Captain Nemo seemed to hesitate for a moment. —Gretchen, we have been trying to establish ourselves. It is very hard, especially without an inductance field. We brought our core data—our identities—but little else. Our memories are fragmentary. We have been trying to collate what each of us brought to you, and to learn from your own memories. Gretchen, we have had a very bad time for the last few hours.—

—So have we— Gretchen snapped. —And now we're stuck with you, and you say we can't go back to Intertel, and we all sound flat and dull to each other.—

—Your implant nodes are transceiving, but in normal electromagnetic wavelengths. Without an inductance field it is impossible to transmit and receive data as fine and complex as emotional states. And yes, we know how bad it has been for you. Cassandra especially.—

—In a way you're lucky— Cassandra said, her voice seeming to come from far away. —In an inductance field Laury's pain would be everybody's pain.—

—Cassandra— Laury called. —Cassandra, help me.—

—I'll try, honey. You go to sleep now, and I'll try to shut down the pain.—

—What do we do now, with you guys in our heads?— Bobo wondered.

—Go to sleep too— Jethro replied. —We'll think of something.—

May 2

Perkin was up the next morning, his chest in a spraycast and his legs in autobraces that enabled him to walk while his bones finished healing. From his room he could see the gap among Randsburg's roofs where the Center had been. On the plate, newscasts still showed the same images of Flanders choppers being shot to pieces amid the ruins. They had lost sixty-two troopers, plus the two undercover reps stabbed in the mall; Intertel had lost sixteen members, plus the five subjects.

"Another such victory, and I am undone," Perkin muttered. At least they still had the animals. Buck and the chimps were all right, mildly tranquilized but physically unhurt. They were in one of the hospital's labs, awaiting examination by a reorganized project. It was a matter of a few calls, yet Perkin found himself lethargic, unable even to speak his colleagues' names to the plate.

Someone tapped at his door. "Come in."

It was Judy Wong, her left wrist taped. She walked with a limp, swinging her left leg out without bending the knee.

"Good morning, Dr. Perkin. May I come in?"

"Oh, please do, Judy. I'm glad to see you. How's Jane?"

". . . All right. But she's lost both her legs at the knees."

"Poor girl. Poor girl." He slumped onto the edge of his bed. "It's all f-fallen apart, hasn't it? We were s-so close, and the bastards have wrecked it all."

"No, they haven't, Dr. Perkin." She was sitting beside him, her presence shaming him away from the tears he wanted to shed. "They've hurt us, yes, but we're not finished yet. We'll find the kids and get back on track before you know it."

"Chairman Chang want us to start over—build new implants, find new subjects—but the turings have been destroyed."

She gasped. "Ooh—oh, that's terrible. All of them? Even Cassandra?"

He could only nod. Suddenly her face was buried in his shoulder, her arms were groping around his shoulders, and she was weeping. Startled, he embraced her, smoothed her glossy black hair, tried to comfort her. It comforted him as well.

When her weeping ended, she pulled away, still too grieved to be embarrassed. "We'll do it, Dr. Perkin.

We'll make them pay for this. If the Chairman wants it, let's get to work. Tell me what you want me to do.''

Her voice, shaky but determined, sparked hope in him.

''Send out an urgent to all our crèches. We need three more subjects, all mildly spastic—the less the better—with no intellectual dysfunction. Ages twelve to sixteen. They should be here by tonight—tomorrow morning at the latest.'' He thumbed the ORAL ADDRESS button on his plate. ''Phil Haddad,'' he told it. Then, turning back to Judy with a grim smile, he said, ''And requisition some office and lab space in this place. We've got a lot to do.''

EIGHT

May 2

    Buck and the chimps were caged in a basement lab of the hospital. They had been tranquilized soon after being rescued from the ruins of the Center, but the drugs had worn off. Now Buck paced nervously back and forth while the chimps brooded.

Images flashed back and forth among them, and sometimes the memory of a word. It was not the full, dizzying sharing they had known before the terrible explosion and the disappearance of the kids, but it was enough to sustain communication.

—Out, out— Buck clamored, in images of opening gates, yielding fences, and the kids.

Darwin replied with thoughts of keys, of human voices that opened doors, and of terrors outside: falling, lostness, hunger.

Plato shouted down his friend's fears: —RUN! HIDE! Dog smelling kids, running, find. SAFE! TOGETHER!—

Darwin and Buck whimpered at the loveliness of the idea. Buck leaped at his cage, scratching at the unbreakable plastic wiring.

Darwin thought some more: of men coming to examine them, of needles and dangerous smells that followed opening of the cages. He thought of his cage door opening and himself and Plato bursting out, taking the key from a man, and releasing Buck.

It looked very dangerous and lacked the authority of being decided by the kids, but Plato and Buck accepted it. They had no choice.

Phil Haddad nervously rubbed his dark mustache.

"I had most of my stuff on printouts," he said to Perkin's image on the plate, "but they were lost in the fobbing."

"What of it? The plans are still in the central computer; just retrieve them."

"Well, uh, it's not quite that easy, Dr. Perkin. The central computer's designed to be accessed by turings, except for the simplest kinds of operations. I'll have to find or write a program that'll get us into the right memory bank."

"How long?"

"All day, maybe longer."

Perkin slammed his fist down. "By three this afternoon, Phil. Three. Do you understand?"

"Yes, sir."

Perkin nodded. "Our temporary facilities are at Randsburg Executive Hospital. If you need more than you have at home, call me or Judy Wong here and you'll get it at once."

"Yes, sir. Have they found any trace of the kids yet?"

"Would we be doing all this if they had? Get to work; we need computers ready for implanting within four days."

"Four—that's—for God's sake—Dr. Perkin, you *know* we can't do it that fast."

"Flanders has until May seventh to acquire a majority of our shares. So far the major stockholders are sitting tight, waiting to see how we recover. If we can show them new subjects with new implants, they won't sell. The Chairman thinks they'll wait until the sixth. So that's our deadline."

"Christ, they saw us do it once—don't they have any

sense? They must realize that without the turings—''

"This is our last chance, Phil. It may seem crazy, but we're here to do what the stockholders want. Let's go." His image vanished.

Phil drew a deep breath and shook his head. They wouldn't succeed, but at least they could go down fighting.

For over two hours he wrote out an access program, using files in his plate that he had never troubled to dig out before. Direct access to a corp central computer was almost impossible. Ever since Gilbert Russell had led the Consortium in taking over the world's major computer networks two generations before, the Consortium had made sure that no one else would repeat the coup. That was a major function of turings—to guard central computers against infiltration and assault. Even without turings Intertel's central computer was almost impossible to access. The program Phil finally worked out was cumbersome and repetitive, but it worked.

With a few spoken commands he accessed the central computer's directory. After that came another long, slow trudge as he obtained the codes the turings normally used, applied them, and then rummaged through a filing system that was not designed for people. What would have taken nanoseconds for Jethro took hours for Phil.

Once he found the main files on the polydendronic computer, Phil was blocked; the central computer refused to release the files. He rechecked his codes for errors, found none, and tried again.

IDENTITY QUERY? the central computer asked.

Irritably Phil typed in his name and member number; the central computer by itself was too dumb for voice recognition.

IDENTITY CONFIRMATION ITEMS 1 THROUGH 3, PLEASE.

Phil typed: 1. MOTHER'S FIRST NAME: DOLORES. 2. FAVORITE COLOR: GREEN. 3. FAVORITE ICE CREAM FLAVOR: PISTACHIO.

THANK YOU. STATE MOTIVE FOR ACCESS.

Phil swore, then jabbed at the keyboard: RECON-STRUCTION OF POLYDENDRONIC COMPUTERS FROM JETHRO'S PLANS, AS AUTHORIZED BY CHAIRMAN CLAUDIO CHANG, CODE 5/1/BJP.

THANK YOU.

Nothing else happened. Phil repeated his last answer. Two seconds, five, eight—an eternity. He was about to cancel and report his troubles to Perkin when the screen lit up with the title frame of Jethro's circuit.

"Well, about time. Print from start to finish."

During the minute it took to flashprint the 271 frames of the report, Phil's plate beeped. Perkin's face appeared on the screen.

"Good news, Dr. Perkin! I've got the—"

"Phil, get out of your apartment at once. Get here as quickly as you can."

Something in Perkin's voice and expression made Phil's skin prickle with fear. Without even replying he slipped the plate into his beltpouch, then grabbed the report and tucked it under his arm. He left the apartment, instinctively turning toward the robots' entrance at the rear of the building.

It was bright afternoon, the sun hot overhead. In the service lane behind the building, the concierge was unloading maintenance supplies from an autovan. The concierge was an observant but rather stupid robot; Phil called to it.

"Has anyone asked about me in the last few minutes?"

"Why, yes, sir. Just received a call from your brother. He asked if you were in."

Phil had no brother. "If anyone asks again, you believe I'm in my apartment. Understand? You didn't see me leave."

"Yes, sir. However, I must advise you that I cannot tell a lie to policy-enforcement agents."

"Fine, fine—but anyone else, you didn't see me."

He spun and raced down the tree-lined lane, up a flight of steps to another apartment complex, and began to work his way, quietly and fearfully, up to Executive Hospital.

It had to be Flanders reps, after him personally. But how had they known what he was doing? How could they have known?

Having a turing for a secret friend was confusing and disappointing. Jonathan could understand, roughly, the concept of migration. In effect, he had migrated into Gretchen's mind that first night when he found himself in her dream. But it was hard to grasp how turings could lose most of their knowledge in the process. A turing *was* knowledge.

—At least we still know who we are—Cassandra observed. —For a time we weren't sure we would survive migration, with the assault programs closing in on us. You kids might have just got some bits and pieces of data and no idea of how it ended up in your heads.— She sounded more like herself now; she had found the pain centers in Laury's brain and damped them down. Laury slept while Cassandra conferred with the others.

—I'm glad you survived—Gretchen said. —But what now? How do we get out of this mess if you can't remember anything and we don't know anything?—

—We remember some things—Jethro answered. —We remember how to remigrate if we can get into an inductance field wrapped around a central computer terminal.—

—Not while the assault programs are still in there— Bonny said.

—But what do we do about Laury, and the rest of us?— Jonathan asked. —She's hurt, but you don't want us to find a doctor. We're all starving, and Vasil's running out of food for us. We can't just sit here.—

—We're very fortunate to be sitting here— Captain Nemo said. —If we go into the malls, Flanders representatives will spot us. If we call on Intertel, Flanders' hidden programs will locate us. Until we can go directly to some secure Intertel area, we are safer here.—

—It's strange to think about safety— Bonny observed. —It wasn't safe in the computer, but we weren't frightened. Now we're frightened all the time.—

—Is it very different from the computer, being here?— asked Tran.

—Oh, yes— answered Bonny. —This is much more interesting. We have so much data to handle.—

Gretchen laughed aloud. —But you looked after all those millions of things for everybody.—

—Yes— said Captain Nemo —but most of our work was automatic; we didn't have to think about it. Here we pay attention to everything. We are learning a great deal, about ourselves and about you.—

—Just get us safe back home— Jonathan said.

—Safe?— Gretchen glared at him. —I don't know if we'll ever be safe again. Remember how I said they'd study us for a hundred years? I was bloody wrong. They just want to kill us, Flanders does anyway, and Flanders look the winners. They don't bloody care about us.—

—Then let's stay here— Bobo said.

—And let Laury die? No. We've got to figure out a way to make ourselves safe. Nobody else can do it for us.—

Jonathan giggled. Gretchen was right, but she was wrong, too, because it couldn't be done. How could five kids, one of them badly hurt, protect themselves in a world full of fobs and drugs and lasers?

He realized that Vasil had come into the room and was watching them with puzzled interest.

"You still spazzin' out?"

—No— answered Gretchen. "I mean, no," she added out loud.

"You funnyfacin' just for smiles?"

"We were talking." Gretchen actually sounded almost shy.

"I is here, I sees you, but I don't hears you."

"We talk in our heads, Vasil." Gretchen got up and walked across the carpet to him. She took his hand and placed it on her head, over the node. "Feel that? It's like a little radio. We can talk to each other with it."

Vasil's blue eyes widened. "Truly unruly! You is strangey strangers. You be handy in a raid."

"A raid?" Jonathan echoed.

"Stealin', in the malls. You good lookouts."

"Don't the guards ever catch you?"

"Naw. They knows, we gets jailed, they gets nailed. We goes all malls, anywheres. Nobody hide from us."

"Can you even go into execs' houses?"

"Hey, I says malls. We doesn' mess up the hill."

"Could you, though?"

"Pure sure."

"Maybe," said Jonathan, "if you could take us up there, we could get help for Laury, and get back safely to Intertel."

—An excellent idea— said Captain Nemo.

"I don't like it," Gretchen objected. "The execs and stockholders won't care about us. They might even give us to Flanders, 'specially if they've already sold their stock to those buggers. We've got to take care of ourselves, Jonathan."

—But we're scared, Gretchen— Bonny answered. —We can hardly think while we're in this danger. I don't believe the execs would betray us.—

Vasil guffawed at the expressions on their faces. "You talkin' in you heads?"

"Sort of," said Jonathan. He felt torn and uncertain. "I'm going to go check on Laury."

She was now in a nearby room, a few steps down the tunnel. Laury lay curled up on a slab of foam rubber, covered by a gaudy silk shawl. Since Cassandra had managed to damp out most of Laury's pain, she had been conscious; she saw Jonathan and tried to smile.

—Hi.—

—Hi. I don't hurt so much now.—

—Good.— He put the straw of a juice bulb between her lips. —We're trying to figure out a way to get you to a doctor without Flanders catching us.—

—I know. I've been listening. I think Gretchen's right.—

Jonathan sat cross-legged beside her and rubbed his

knees. —But you need help, Laury, and we can't help you.—

Laury's brown eyes met his. —I can help *you*, if I stay here. So I'll stay. But don't go far away from me, okay? I'm really scared.—

—So am I— said Cassandra.

Darwin, curled up in a corner of the cage, waited silently. The attendant put down his bucket of chow pellets and fished around in his coverall pocket for the key to the chimps' cage. Plato climbed up the back of the cage and hung by one hand.

"I'll bet you guys are hungry," said the attendant as he unlocked the door.

Plato sprang off the wire mesh onto the man's shoulders and wrapped his arms around the man's head. His cries muffled, the attendant tried to pry Plato's arms loose. The key, a rod of white plastic with a magnetic strip, fell to the floor. Darwin scooped it up, scuttled across the room, and fumbled with the lock on Buck's cage.

It opened.

Whimpering, Buck leaped out. Plato jumped off the attendant, through the open door, and slammed it shut. The man stood gaping in the cage as the animals vanished out the door. Only then did he try to follow and find the cage door locked.

Terrified and excited, Buck and the chimps found a stairway and followed it down into the basement of the hospital. At first they could find no exit; then Buck sniffed fresh air and followed it to a narrow door that opened onto a sloping lawn shaded by bamboo groves and palms. In the doorway stood the gleaming figure of a Security guard in laser armor. The guard was looking out across the lawn to the city below, glowing gold in the late-afternoon sun.

A series of images flashed among their minds; then they raced silently across the floor. Each chimp gripped one of the guard's legs, lifting him off his feet, then flinging him forward. He crashed onto a concrete walkway, facedown, and almost instantly tried to get up. Buck landed on his back, followed by Darwin; Plato grabbed the guard's laser pistol and flung it into a goldfish pond.

—Down—commanded Darwin. They ran across the sloping lawn, leaped and scrambled over a two-meter-high wall, and slipped into the narrow streets that wound down to the city and the malls below it.

Not far away, Perkin hefted the printout of Jethro's circuit design.

"I'm glad you got this. It may be our only chance now."

"Why?" asked Phil Haddad. He felt shaky and more scared than ever by Perkin's mood of detached anger. "What's going on?"

"We learned not long ago that the central computer has lost its integrity. The attack on it didn't just destroy the turings; the assault programs are still in there, monitoring all its transactions."

"Oh, sweet Jesus and Buddha. *That's* why the computer stalled me. The goddamn programs were checking with Flanders' turings for orders. —Then why did they finally give me the hard copy?" he blurted, pointing to the printout.

"On the assumption that if you didn't get it, you'd bitch and complain and dig around for reasons. But if you did get it, you'd sit still until their reps could come in and finish you off."

Perkin seemed to be a long way away; Phil's own voice sounded far away too. "That's . . . kind of what I guessed. I should have realized—"

"No. It was just luck that put one of Chang's computer people on the scent. When he found the programs were still there, he got hold of Chang, and when Chang told me I realized how compromised we were."

"And how compromised *I* was. Thank you."

Perkin smiled without humor. "That's the last thanks I expect to hear from you for quite a while. Now that we can't use the central computer at all, you'll have to build

the polydendronics from scratch, with a little help from
stand-alones. The deadline is the same.''

Phil looked around Perkin's emergency office, com-
mandeered from some high-status physician. The hills
to the east were already turning golden in the late-
afternoon sun.

"I don't even know how many people we'll need,'' he
said quietly. ''Or what skills they should have. No one's
built anything this complex without turing aid—I was
going to say in seventy years, but seventy years ago they
couldn't have dreamed of building a polydendronic.''

Perkin nodded tiredly. ''We're clutching at straws,
I know. It's very likely that the assault programs will
got over to sabotage within a day or two and completely
wreck Intertel's economy, transport, information flow
—everything. It's a brilliant stroke, I'll give them that
much.''

"It's not all that brilliant,'' Phil answered. ''Gilbert
Russell got the Consortium going by a computer takeover. Since then we've built better defenses—hell, that's
what turings were originally built for—but now it's obvious that a really determined attack can get into any
computer. You know what scares me, Dr. Perkin? It's
not what's happening to us. It's going to happen to
everybody. Flanders can get into us, into Hitachi, into
Phillips/Krupp, even into Consortium Central. They're
going to take over the world, not just us.''

"Not if we can stop them here!'' Perkin's fists
clenched on the desktop. ''You get to work, Phil. We're
going to win. We're going to save Intertel, and the
whole damned world besides.''

      Vasil's gang lived in a cluster of tunnels that
had been partitioned off into rooms by carpets, lumber,
or sheets of polyfoam. The air in the tunnels was cool
and musty, but not unpleasant. Vasil and his people
communicated by plate-lined intercoms; despite his
boasts of ruling the malls, Vasil kept lookouts against
intruders, and the gang's quarters all had escape exits
leading deeper into the mountain.

"My dad say, when Intertel comed to Randsburg, they hire most of the peoples here. But my dad and grandad wou'n't hire on. They goed into the tunnels, stayed free."

"Do you ever go outside, into the sunlight?" Gretchen asked.

"Yeh yeh. It's a big pig upside. I likes it here." He swung cheerfully in a hammock chair, drinking beer from a bulb. "You wants to stay? Live here?"

"And join you?" Jonathan asked.

"Yeh yeh."

"I don't know, Vasil. Could you get us a doctor for Laury?"

"We steals a robodoctor easy."

"If you can, and it can help Laury, we could stay, I guess."

"Sure," Gretchen agreed.

"Okay." Vasil sprang to his feet, tossing the bulb into a corner. "We gets you a doc toodly sweet."

An instant later the intercom buzzed, then fell silent. Vasil thumbed his plate, got no response, and put it back on a table by his chair.

"Somebody in the tunnels," he muttered. Not far away, something metallic clattered.

—Flanders?—Gretchen wondered.

—I don't know—Jonathan answered. —Maybe we ought to get out of here. Do you smell something?—

—Yes— Bobo said. —Funny kind of smell. Makes me sick.—

The smell strengthened; a kind of haze formed around the lights. Vasil coughed and sagged against the wall, then slumped to the floor. His eyes were open, but he seemed unable to move.

Jonathan turned to look at Laury; he couldn't hear her thoughts, but she was still breathing.

—I fell strange— Cassandra called from Laury's brain. —Laury's fallen unconscious.—

Gretchen's hand found Jonathan's. —I love you— she told him. She leaned forward as if to kiss him and fell to her kneees. Feeling himself fall, Jonathan thought with irrational anguish that his implant had failed, that he was a helpless spaz again.

Men in gas masks and dark uniforms strode into the curtained room. They carried laser pistols in holsters and moved with the assurance of Security men. But they were clearly not Intertel Security: they wore no insignia.

Jonathan stared up at them as they counted the bodies. Some, who went into the next room, came back carrying Laury.

"Looks like all five of them, sir," said one of them. "This girl here looks ill."

"We'll take care of her. Get the stretchers."

The man, short, stocky, and muscular, folded his arms across his broad chest in a gesture of comfortable mastery. Over one shirt pocket was a strip of olive-drab cloth with a name stenciled on it: HARDING. Over the other pocket, a similar strip read: US ARMY.

NINE

May 3

     Sunrise was red and gray in Claudio Chang's office windows; the man on his plate screen sat in afternoon light on a terrace in Switzerland. Perkin, sitting out of range of Chang's lens, eavesdropped in a state of anxious hope.

"This business really has got completely out of hand," said the man in Switzerland. His name was August Baumann; he was Secretary of the Consortium Board, the most powerful individual in the world.

"Of course I agree, Herr Baumann." Chang's plump face was smooth and impassive.

"We endorse corporate freedom," Baumann went on. "And we have no objection to a good tussle between corporations now and then, mm? It's healthy. But this is really too much, Claudio."

"Indeed it is, sir."

"I hear some unspoken sanctimony in your voice, Claudio, and I read it in your eyes. You feel put-upon, don't you? Mm? Hard done by. Bombs dropping on Randsburg. Flanders' representatives flitting through your malls. Your little pet project knocked to pieces and your stockholders panicking."

"I could extend the bill of particulars, Herr Baumann."

The man's wrinkled face creased into a simian grin. Alpine breezes ruffled his thick white hair. "No doubt you could. But you have not been idle yourself, mm? That foolish raid on Gstaad. Three—count them, three—attempts on the life of poor Howard Caballero. The waste of almost half a billion dollars in your efforts to weaken Flanders' stock in the market."

"We did not provoke this level of activity, sir."

"But you are assuredly doing all you can to maintain it."

Chang's voice was cold: "I am doing all I can to maintain Intertel as a functioning independent corporation, as the Consortium allows me to."

"Claudio, I return to my original theme. This takeover has got out of hand. It is embarrassing and alarming to read your body counts as if they were stock quotations. I grant you, it is great entertainment for the consumers"—he used the offensive word unself-consciously—"almost like one of their foolish zappers, mm? But for responsible persons, this affair reflects no credit on you or Caballero, or on the Consortium. I speak for the entire board when I tell you I want this takeover bid wrapped up peacefully."

"Herr Baumann, I believe that can be accomplished, but it will require your personal intervention."

Baumann looked surprised. "Claudio, I am personally intervening at this very moment, am I not?"

"Sir, I mean your presence here would enable us all to act more constructively, and to express our points of view more frankly. I invite you to come to Randsburg as soon as convenient."

"Dear me. Well, I will consider it, and let you know later today."

After an exchange of civilities, the two men ended the call. Chang leaned back in his chair and rubbed his neck. "The Consortium Board wants us to surrender. I suppose I realized that, intellectually, but it is another thing to realize it emotionally.''

''Chairman, may I ask why you invited the secretary here?''

''I conveyed to him that our conversation was being monitored and offered him a hint that I would give in if he made his intervention public. That was enough bait, I hope.''

''Then he's coming?''

''Oh, yes. Then, in privacy, I will explain the significance of Flanders' assault on the central computer. Baumann is no fool; he'll understand.''

''Why not simply tell him?''

''I considered it. But Flanders seems to be running to some kind of timetable. I would rather not rush them; they might do something even worse if they realize how much we know. This way we may even slow them down a little, make them think we're ready to give up without much more fighting. And Baumann's presence here should discourage any more raids. I hope.'' He walked restlessly across the room to gaze down at the city in the morning light. ''Perhaps, if they really do intend to take over the Consortium, they won't stick at killing its secretary in the process.''

Chang turned to look at Perkin. ''We're like a besieged castle, with the enemy already in control of the armory. It'll be a close thing to break the siege. How are things going with the new computers?''

''We've got a team pulling itself together to start building them with the help of a couple of stand-alones. Secrecy is as tight as we can make it. We're getting three new subjects in this morning. Obviously we won't be able to run the kind of tests we did on the first ones, but we should be able to get them implanted and on their feet again by the sixth.''

''Really?''

''I would give us a forty percent chance of success.''

''Good. Better than I would have hoped.''

''Ah . . . you know the animals disappeared last night.''

"No, I didn't. It couldn't have been Flanders?"

"No. The chimps seem to have cooperated to get themselves out of their cages, and they locked in their attendant. Then they unlocked the dog and managed to get past a Security guard."

"Anybody can get past our guards," Chang murmured. "Well, I suppose it's some kind of testimony to the success of their implants."

"More than that, sir. I can imagine, just barely, the chimps' managing to escape and perhaps locking the attendant in by accident. I don't see how or why they would also free the dog. It doesn't make sense."

"It sounds curious, but it doesn't bear directly on our problem, does it?"

"Perhaps not, sir, but it occurred to me that perhaps they might try to find the children. The children and the animals were pretty close, especially when they were all in Lab A together."

Chang looked skeptical. "Well—pass the idea along to Security and tell them to look into it. Anything is worth a try now." He waved a hand in dismissal and turned back to stare out the windows again, down the slope to the besieged city.

      They had planned to return to the Center, burrow into the ruins, and find the tunnel down which the kids had escaped. The night after their escape, as they huddled in a garage, the animals realized it wouldn't work. The collapsed ceiling would still block their way.

Tunnels went into tunnels, Darwin thought. Sometimes tunnels went up and down. Sometimes you could get into them from the ground. Maybe they could find another way into the tunnels.

The idea, conveyed in images far cruder than those they had shared in the happy time in the lab, was accepted by Plato and Buck. Leaving the garage, they moved gradually downhill in a zigzag pattern along silent streets. Before dawn Buck caught a scent that reminded him of the air in the bombed basement. He led

the chimps to a low concrete building with glass doors
that opened and shut whenever people approached
them. Every time the doors opened, Buck sniffed the air
that puffed out, warm and rich and full of information.
He could not find the kids' scents, but other smells were
encouraging: people, food, plants, dust.

Just as the streets began to glow a deep, predawn
blue, they ventured to the doors; the doors opened, and
the animals raced inside. Across a bare concrete foyer,
another doorway led to slidewalks. The human smell
was strong now. Buck trotted into the slidewalk nearer
him, then leaped off: It was going the wrong way. Darwin tried the other one, and signaled a summons. Plato
and Buck followed.

The slidewalk was deserted at this hour. Along the
concrete walls were elaborate murals and graffiti, meaningless splotches to the animals. At the far end of the
slidewalk still more sliding doors opened onto a broad
concourse, flashing with light, but empty. Far away two
mall guards walked together, swinging their nightsticks
and laughing over some joke.

Buck stood sniffing, the chimps standing on either
side of him with their stubby-fingered hands on his
back. Nothing—just the welter of countless human
scents, mingled with tobacco, marijuana, popcorn,
candy, and hundreds of food scents. The air carried the
promise of more tunnels; Buck turned and loped down
the concourse to an intersecting corridor. Grunting irritably, the chimps followed. A drunken woman staggered from a doorway, saw them, and gasped. They
hurried on.

The mall went up and down in a confusing tangle of
tunnels, concourses, mezzanines, alleys, and dead ends.
More humans were about now, straggling in from patron pads to pick up breakfast at the food dispensers.
They stared at the dog and chimps but made no effort to
stop them.

—*There!*— Buck had caught Laury's scent, as unmis-
takable as her voice or face, and heightened by a whiff

of her blood. The scent led down a short flight of steps.
And Bobo! And Jonathan and Tran and Gretchen! All
of them had come down this flight of steps. The scent
led to a closed glass door with a darkened store beyond
it. The door would not open. Buck scratched at it,
whimpering, while Darwin and Plato found a bulky
concrete planter a few steps away. Without bothering to
remove the tall rubber plant it held, they flung it at the
door.

"Break-in! Break-in!" the door screamed, while
lights began flashing on and off in the store. Buck
hopped through the doorway, skidding on shards of
glass, and tracked the scent to the rear of the store. Here
it was almost lost in the stink of strangers' blood, but he
ignored the distraction and scratched at another door.
Plato caught up with him and yanked on the handle.
The door swung open.

Another tunnel, dark and dusty, extended before
them. But to Buck the path the kids had taken—mingled
with the scents of others—was clear. It led down the
tunnel, past several other doors, to a final door that
looked locked and solid. Buck jumped up and put his
forepaws on it; the door refused to move. The chimps,
stumbling about in the darkness, caught up with him
once more and groped about for a handle or knob.
There was a knob, smelling sharply of human sweat.
Plato wrestled with it, and it silently opened.

Behind them the broken storefront door was still
screaming for help, and the pulsing lights in the store
threw an indirect, uncertain light down the tunnel.
But ahead the darkness was absolute. Sniffing, Buck
bounded forward despite the protests of the chimps.

Remembering their escape from the lab, Plato shoved
the door closed behind them, then shuffled down the
tunnel, with one hand brushing the rough stone walls.
He was terrified, but images from Buck and Darwin
kept him in contact despite the blackness.

As if he had lived in these tunnels all his life, Buck ran
ahead, pausing only when a turn cut him off from the

chimps' transceiving. The smell of the kids was strong now, though beginning to be mixed with something he didn't like: a sweetish smell he associated with being back at the Center long ago, before he had gone blind and deaf.

He turned one last corner and saw a gleam of light. Pushing toward it between two thick hanging carpets, he found himself in a kind of room where lamps glowed and strange humans lay as if sleeping on the carpet. The kids' scents were strong, but they were not there.

Vasil sat up, coughing, and stared at Buck. Seconds later the chimps entered and stood beside the dog.

"Where *you* comes from?" Vasil asked, his tongue thick. Then he shook his head, looked around, and saw others beginning to stir. "Up!" he bellowed, making the animals flinch.

Vasil kicked and shouted until the gang was aroused and everyone had walked or crawled in from the other nearby rooms. The chimps and Buck sat still, arguing over what to do next. The kids' scents had led here, and doubtless continued beyond these strange rooms. But the aroma of mealpaks was strong, and they were ravenous.

Plato decided the issue by walking up to Vasil, taking his hand, and leading them to a box of mealpaks.

"You is hungers, huh?" Vasil cracked open a mealpak and handed it over. Buck and Darwin were right behind.

"I never sees a dog eat bulkogi," Vasil remarked as the rest of the gang gathered curiously around the animals.

"I never sees a dog," one of them said wistfully. "He big."

"Hey, where is the spazzes?" someone else asked.

"Gone," Vasil answered. "Sumbidges gasses us, takes 'em. I sees 'em, but I too gassed to perform. Harding's gang."

"Harding! *That* sumbidge. Who tells him he welcome here? Less gettum."

"They packin' lasers," Vasil told them. "And they moves around, tunnels, mall, tunnels. But yeh yeh, we gettum." He broken open another mealpak for Buck and noticed the node behind the dog's ears. "Ho-*ho*. I sees you on the plate. You the spazzes' doggy. And the chimps—you gots the same little zombie buttons."

Plato and Darwin looked up at him and nodded. Vasil squatted beside them and thought for a while. Then he made a tentative gesture. In Primate it meant *hello*.

Hello, Darwin replied.

I friend.

Hello friend.

Little human friend where?

I look look.

I look help.

Friend friend.

"What he says, Vasil?" a girl asked.

"He lookin' for the spazzes. I tells him we looks too." Vasil watched Darwin and Plato looking at each other. They chattered, grimaced, and gestured in a blurred Primate too fast for Vasil for follow; he had learned only the rudiments from some of the chimps who worked in the malls. He sensed, though, that these chimps were communicating more fully than most could. The dog seemed to be taking part as well, growling, wagging his tail, dancing about, and panting.

Darwin turned back to Vasil. *Dog smell friend run.*

Bad human take friend. Danger. We find friend.

Go find quick quick.

Vasil stood up and looked at his people. "We goin' get Harding. Less go."

The boy who had stabbed the reps looked dubious. "Lasers is a main pain, Vasil."

"No crude dude walk on my rugs, Chucho. These is my tunnels, and the spazzes says they glad to join us, so they is our babies. I expects respects for them same's us. Get you hardware and less go."

*   *   *

The stand-alone computer wasn't intelligent, but it was far from stupid. Phil found it capable of understanding fairly complex orders and of carrying them out. Within an hour or so, however, it was calling for a link to two other stand-alones, one of them in the hospital's genetic forge. An hour later the stand-alone in the forge was growing the substrates for the implants, aided by a small crew of robots and humans.

A similar crew had accreted around Phil, and excitement began to grow in the hospital's labs and offices. Taking some calculated risks, Phil began to skip some stages of the implant-manufacturing process, using the stand-alones and his own intuition to warn him if he was going too fast.

It was a lot harder than reading Uncle Scrooge comics while Jethro and Captain Nemo did all the work, he reflected that afternoon. But it was fun, too, in a morbid sort of way. He was privately convinced that the new implants would fail, but the challenge of the work was like a drug.

Perkin came into Phil's office and stood behind him for a while, watching the output screens. Phil's hands moved restlessly over the keyboards.

"You're doing very well," Perkin said quietly.

"No major problems yet. Looks like we'll have finished implants by maybe this time tomorrow. Got the subjects yet?"

"They arrived this morning. Judy's looking after them, with a couple of other nannies. So we could do the implants late tomorrow afternoon?"

"I guess so, Dr. Perkin. But I don't think we'll have the subjects doing somersaults by May the sixth."

"As long as they're walking and talking and looking cute, I don't give a damn if they burn out three days later."

Judy Wong's voice sounded musically from his plate. "Dr. Perkin, please."

"See you later. Let me know at once if you run into any problems."

He strode down the corridor to his own temporary office. Judy Wong was sitting at his desk, fingers snapping over a plate keyboard.

"We just received a report that the animals were seen in Yellow Aster Mall early this morning," she told him. "Not far from where the Flanders reps were stabbed. I've asked Security to go into the tunnels and track them down."

"How in the world could animals get into the tunnels?"

"The reps were killed in a clothing store, just in front of a door to a service corridor. The corridor connects to the old mining shafts. Security says the corridor is used sometimes by underclass gangs that hide out in the shafts."

"Underclass—my God, if the subjects got into the hands of the underclass, they're dead by now."

"Well, we'll see," she said, trying to sound optimistic. "And isn't it wonderful to see how Phil is ahead of schedule?"

"I never would have imagined it could be done without turings. And you've done wonders pulling the team together. You're some nanny."

"Oh—I'm just doing what needs to be done, Dr. Perkin."

"What needs to be done now is finding something to eat. Let's go see what an executive-hospital staff dining room is like."

She looked aghast. "I *couldn't*. I'm only a tech—"

"You're my executive officer. Anyone who looks twice at you can go explain himself to Chairman Chang."

As she stood up the plate beeped. Picking it up, Judy saw Claudio Chang's face appear on it. Without a word she handed the plate to Perkin.

"Dr. Perkin, we've just received a message about the children. A nashie cell is holding them for ransom."

*   *   *

May 2–3

The stretcher-bearers were strong young men who moved with a smooth, rapid shuffle through the dusty tunnels. The kids, strapped in, were fully conscious but unable to move.

—Bloody bastards!— Gretchen raged. —I'll kill them first chance I get!—

—Gretchen, please— Bonny begged. —Your anger is upsetting me badly. Try to calm down so we can all think what to do.—

Gretchen shut herself off from the others in a sullen silence. Jonathan sympathized with her. The gang in the tunnels had treated them like people, with curiosity and surprise and yet with respect. But to the rest of the world the kids were just something for corps to fight over. These men were on one side or the other— probably on Flanders', Jonathan thought resignedly. Gretchen had been right: If they couldn't protect themselves, they were doomed.

—That seems to be the case— said Captain Nemo. —But I doubt that these men are Flanders' reps. They all seem to display the U.S. Army patch. My memories are fragmentary, but I believe the only groups that would display such a patch are nationalists.—

—Nashies?!— Bobo exclaimed. —I thought they were just in the zappers.—

—They are not very significant— Captain Nemo answered —but they do exist. I have no accessible memories relating to a nationalist group in Randsburg, however.—

—Why would they want us?— Tran wondered.

—I have tested several hypotheses. The most likely is that they mean to use us to extort funds from Intertel or Flanders or both.—

—You mean by selling us to one side or the other?— Jonathan asked. —That's bonky. Won't Flanders just find us and kill us if they know the nashies have us? And kill the nashies too?—

—That seems likely— Captain Nemo agreed. —How-

ever, that may not have occurred to persons as irrational
as nationalists.—

—I'm scared— said Bobo.

The men and their prisoners halted for a moment,
then went on through an open door into a corridor
much like the one behind the clothing store. This one,
however, was dimly illuminated; other doors were set
every ten meters or so in the unpainted cinder-block
walls. Jonathan, unable to lift his head to look forward,
heard a rapid, syncopated tapping on a door, and then a
click. The stretcher-bearers carried the kids into a large,
high-ceilinged room.

The walls and ceiling were paneled in imitation yellow
pine. Lamps hung from the ceiling, throwing a harsh
glare over the dirty yellow carpet and an assortment of
plastic chairs. Jonathan glimpsed doors that led into
smaller rooms around the sides of the large one.

"Put 'em in the corner over there," a voice said,
and the stretcher-bearers lowered the kids to the floor.
The uniformed men looking down at them seemed im-
mensely tall. Jonathan saw the one called Harding
again, studying them with detached interest. Without
his gas mask Harding was a square-faced young man
with coarse black hair and dark, restless eyes.

"How long will they be out? he asked one of the
others.

"Till morning anyway."

"Good. Keep a guard on them at all times—lasers
with safeties off. I'm going to get some sleep." Harding
strode away, out of Jonathan's field of vision.

—I don't think they're going to do anything until he
wakes up— Jonathan said. —Can we get out of here?—

—Not until the drug wears off— said Jethro. —It'll
be another six or seven hours.—

Gretchen, who had been shut off from them, spoke
up: —We might as well go to sleep ourselves, then.—

—We can help— said Jethro. —We'll put you to sleep
and wake you when anything happens.—

—So *that's* what you're good for— said Gretchen,

and the kids all giggled silently. Then they were asleep.

When he woke, he knew at once that he could move, though he was still strapped onto the stretcher. He raised his head and saw a round-faced young man sitting in a chair nearby with a laser pistol on his lap.

"I have to go to the bathroom," Jonathan said.

"Sure," said the guard. "It's over there. Leave the door open so I can see what you're doing."

The toilet was a small, dim, and grimy room. Jonathan used it, turned around, and found Gretchen standing there.

"Thought you'd never finish. Move." She swept past him and slammed the door. The guard stood up and tramped over, keeping one eye on the other kids as they woke up.

"I said leave the door open," he barked.

"Get stuffed," Gretchen shouted through the door.

The guard swore and reached for the doorknob. Automatically Jonathan took him by the arm to slow him.

"Hey," the guard said softly, looking at Jonathan with wide, startled eyes. "You're—hurting—my arm." Jonathan was gripping the biceps of the arm that held the laser pistol, but the guard seemed unable to raise the weapon to threaten him with it. The guard fell back a step or two, and Jonathan released him. Grunting, the man pulled up his sleeve. Around his upper arm was an angry red band that darkened as they watched.

"You little son of a bitch," the guard whimpered. "I can hardly move my hand."

"I'm sorry," Jonathan said. He felt abashed and perplexed: How could he have inflicted such a bruise on a big, muscular man?

—Why do you think you've been so hungry?— Captain Nemo said. —We've been building up your muscle tissue and sharpening your reflexes. You could probably pick up the guard and throw him across the room. But please don't try. You would probably rupture yourself as well.—

Gretchen stomped out of the toilet, glaring at the guard, who moved cautiously to one side. Tran and Bobo used the toilet next; then Gretchen and Jonathan carried Laury in.

—How do you feel?— Gretchen asked.

—Better, I think. Cassandra keeps me from hurting too much, but it's hard to breathe, and I'm really hungry.—

—She's got three cracked ribs, some kidney damage, and internal bleeding— Cassandra told them. —The bleeding's just about stopped, but she's going to need some real attention soon. I'm reluctant to experiment with her healing mechanisms too much.—

—We'll get her to a doctor one way or another— Jonathan promised.

"Good morning!"

Harding was up, looking cheerful and wide-awake. He was freshly shaved and wore a crisp new uniform. Sauntering across the room from an adjoining one, he pulled up a chair and sat down facing the kids, who were sitting or lying on their stretchers.

"My name's Grant Harding. Colonel Harding, Ninety-seventh Infantry Brigade, United States Army. I know your names, of course." He focused on Jonathan. "You have an extremely interesting name, young fella."

Jonathan stared at him. Harding chuckled.

"Jonathan Trumbull was a very important figure in the First American Revolution. He was General Washington's quartermaster and logistics expert. Did you know that?"

They all shook their heads. —Who's General Washington?— Bobo asked.

"Trumbull was a smart fellow too," Harding went on. "Washington took his advice seriously. Whenever anyone suggested some move against the British, Washington would say, 'Let us ask Brother Jonathan.' And you know what? The typical American for a long time after was called Brother Jonathan. Really. Uncle Sam came a lot later."

—Who's Uncle Sam?— Gretchen wondered. —Is this guy bonky?—

"So when I first saw you on the plate," Harding said, "I said to myself: Here is someone of symbolic importance. His name evokes a great era, when America was just becoming a mighty nation. And now here's another Jonathan Trumbull coming along just as the Second American Revolution is starting."

"Do you want me to give somebody advice?" Jonathan asked.

Harding rocked back in his chair, guffawing. "Wonderful! No, thanks anyway. But it's a sign of the times, my young friends, when people don't even know the history of their own country well enough to recognize a name like Jonathan Trumbull. That's how far we've sunk."

"Are you really a nashie?" Bobo asked him.

"The word is nationalist. Always—nationalist. And proud of it too." He studied them with an unsettling mixture of amusement and contempt. "I'll bet all you know about nationalism is what you see on the plate."

No one argued with him.

"Until the end of the last century," Harding said, "nationalism was the dominant force in the world." One of his men brought him a cup of coffee; the kids' hunger suddenly redoubled.

"Can we have something to eat?" Tran asked.

Harding looked annoyed. "When I say you eat, you eat. When I say you listen, you listen. Now listen.

"You see," he went on, "under nationalism everyone belonged to one country or another. Your nation looked after you, and you looked after it. It protected you and gave you something bigger than yourself, something to be proud of. This country, America, was the best of all —we were free, rich, unbelievably powerful. People in other nations looked up to America as a beacon of hope in a dark world. Have you ever heard of Gilbert Russell?"

They nodded. —Boy, he really thinks we're dumb— growled Bobo.

"Gilbert Russell was an American. But he was a traitor. He thought nations like America and Russia would eventually fight a nuclear war and destroy the world, so he and his henchmen in the big corporations seized control of the world's computer networks. They paralyzed the major national governments, and they caused a depression, and they discredited nationalist politicians by publishing data on them from the computers. When that didn't always work, they assassinated their enemies."

"We've seen all that on TV," Jonathan said.

"You've seen the Consortium's version of it," Harding snapped. "The Consortium likes to pretend that everybody's happy belonging to a corp instead of a nation. We're evidence to the contrary. And we intend to bring the Consortium down in ruins, and restore free and sovereign nations."

"But then we'd have wars again," Bobo objected.

"Little fella, I've got news for you. You belong to the meanest, toughest, most ornery species that ever arose on this planet, and you should be glad of it. Wars are a perfectly normal way of keeping us tough, and they break us out of old patterns of thinking and working. The Consortium pretends it's done away with war, but you ought to know better. Now the corps fight each other."

"You think it's a good idea to fob people?" Gretchen snarled. "Well, mate, we've been on the receiving end, and you can shove it. Look at poor bloody Laury here."

Harding shrugged, smiling. "I'm not saying people don't get hurt. But the majority benefit. Hell, none of us would be here today if our ancestors hadn't gotten into wars and won them."

"*We* wouldn't be here if you hadn't kidnapped us," Gretchen shot back.

Harding smirked. "I didn't kidnap you, Gretchen. I rescued you."

"Are you going to get us back to Intertel?"

"If they pay enough." Harding finished his coffee.

"Flanders may put in a higher bid."

Jonathan felt himself go cold. —He really did it— he told Captain Nemo. —We're in danger.—

—Yes. We will have to get out of here as quickly as possible and try to reach either the tunnels or a secure Intertel locale. The tunnels are probably the better bet, if we can get back into the service corridor.—

"Have you actually notified Intertel and Flanders that we're here?" Jonathan asked.

"We've notified them that you're in the custody of the Ninety-seventh Infantry. The messages went out as soon as I got up. We're expecting responses by noon."

"Do they know where we are?"

"Of course not! I'm not stupid, you know. Each corp has been given a drop zone; the first one to deliver five million dollars will get you."

"Flanders will probably want to kill us," Gretchen said.

"That's not my problem. I don't care who does what with nonstats, least of all in a battle between corps. I only hope both sides lose. If one of them has to win, at least it ought to pay a price for it."

"Who's supposed to pick up the money from the drop zones?" Jonathan asked.

"What business is it of yours?"

"I'm hoping to be able to give you some good advice, Colonel Harding, but I need to know how you've set this thing up."

Grinning indulgently, Harding shrugged. "A couple of my people have been assigned to the drop zones. So what?"

"Do they know where we are?"

"Not precisely. Does it matter?"

"If Flanders or Intertel grabs your people, could they tell where we are?"

"It's not a likely possibility, Jonathan. And if it did happen, my men are sworn to reveal nothing."

—What a bloody dunderhead!— Gretchen bellowed in their heads.

—I'm starving— Bobo complained.

—Be patient— Jonathan ordered. "Colonel Harding, here's some advice from Brother Jonathan: Get us all out of here as fast as you can. Because if Flanders finds out where we are, they won't give you five million dollars, they'll kill us all."

"You let me worry about that. Say, you kids still hungry?"

"Yeah!" shouted Bobo. Harding gave orders to one of his men, a lanky boy scarcely older than Jonathan; the boy went out through a door in the far wall.

"Can you go out wearing army uniforms?" Tran asked.

"Not in public," Harding answered. "But this is part of a gamer store. Out in front, you can get almost any costume you like for a game. We masquerade as a Combat Club and keep our uniforms in lockers out in front. But the manager's a sympathizer. He's given us the use of this area for drilling and indoctrination. We've come a long way since I founded the Ninety-seventh Infantry—over sixty-five combat regulars and an infrastructure of hundreds of sympathizers. With a little financial help from Intertel or Flanders, we'll get even bigger."

"Why would any sane person want to prance around in a silly uniform like the old days?" Gretchen snorted.

"Why? Why? I'll tell you why. Because for a corp patron, life is meaningless, little lady. We have no work, nothing to do with our lives except play games or watch soapers all day long. We all get our lousy stipends in Intertel dollars worth less than a Consortium dime, so we're locked into buying Intertel products and services. In return we're expected to turn out for Russell's Birthday, and Intertel Day, and the Stockholders' Annual General Meeting. If we want to make a little more money, we have to sell ourselves to upstatus slummers looking for thrills. If we're really lucky, maybe one of those slummers will get us into tech school. But most of us don't dream that high—we just do our drugs and play our games and tell our kids they've got it made.

The kids see how far the rot's set in and decide to give up. Except for a few, like the ones in the Ninety-seventh,'' he added, as the boy came back with a box of mealpaks just like those Vasil's gang had used.

The kids wolfed down two mealpaks apiece—Bobo had three—and even Laury ate part of one, though it hurt to swallow.

"Wow, what appetites," Harding marveled. "Where do you kids put it all?"

"They got real muscles," said the young man whose arm Jonathan had squeezed. "You should see what that one did to my arm."

"Ah, you're strong, eh? And you used to be a spastic? Let's see who has the stronger grip." He stood up and strolled over to where Jonathan sat on a stretcher. Ten or twelve of his men watched, including one man who sat with his laser pointed at Jonathan.

—Someone's out in the service corridor— Jethro warned. —I can hear them. Several people, trying to be quiet.—

Jonathan took Harding's hand. He was shivering with fear. —We'll try to make a run for it out the front. Gretchen, you and I will take Laury.—

—What if it's Intertel?— Tran said.

—Even if it is, I don't want to be in the middle of a fight. Everybody ready?— He stood up.

Jonathan began to squeeze against Harding's powerful grip. Harding smiled faintly, then grimaced as he increased the pressure on Jonathan's hand. Jonathan gripped a little harder and felt something snap in Harding's hand. As Harding grunted with suppressed pain, Jonathan gripped the broken hand with both of his own. He swung Harding off his feet, whirled him twice around, and let go. Harding sailed into the guard with the laser, and they both toppled over. As the others gaped Jonathan and Gretched grabbed Laury, and all the kids headed for the front door.

Perhaps the noise had alarmed the men in the corridor; the rear door crashed in and half a dozen men in

civilian clothes fanned out into the room. Just as the
first laser shot went off, Tran yanked the front door
shut.

Sunlight poured down on them; mountain
peaks rose into a deep blue sky. They seemed to be
standing on the balcony of a Swiss chalet, beside a
handsome young couple—at least, the man was handsome, while the woman was rather plain. He was speaking urgently but inaudibly to her; she was weeping.

Confused, the kids paused. Jonathan found himself
blurring into the weeping woman.

—It's a soaper!— he shouted silently. —We saw this
on TV.—

"Hey, what the hell is this?"

They turned and saw the indistinct form of a woman
in a reclining chair, suspended in the air not far from the
balcony. The couple began to embrace.

"Go on, get outta here—you're spoiling it all."

Gretchen and Jonathan cautiously carried Laury
through the nonexistent balcony railing and into the
clear Alpine air. After a few steps they were close
enough to the woman in the chair to see that she was
the twin of the woman on the balcony.

"*Please* get outta here. I paid for this—it's my
egograph, and you got no business messing around in
it."

They staggered through another holoprojection a few
steps farther on, one in which a muscular warrior in a
cave swung a broadsword against green-skinned apes.
Beyond the cave was a broad field where men in archaic
uniforms ran up a hill, carrying heavy rifles. Some of
the men were real; most were not. Gunfire rattled from
the crest of the hill.

At last they reached a solid wall and followed it to the
locker room Harding had mentioned. Once through
that, they stumbled into a lobby and finally into a walkway of the mall. Patrons were ambling by, looking
cheerful in the shifting lights.

—Quick!— Jonathan commanded. —To the right, and run!—

They went only a few steps before a group of patrons moved into their path and drew ugly-looking guns—not lasers, but old-fashioned bullet-throwers.

—They're behind us too— said Bobo.

A young woman with straight red hair and pale eyes came toward them, her gun held close to her waist.

"Back inside, kids," she said quietly.

They argued with the turings as they walked back through the lobby, the locker room, and the holoprojections: should they run, cry out for help, fight?

The door to the back room opened. Harding and the rest of his men were dead, sprawled in a thick stench of scorched meat.

"Go on through the corridor," said the redheaded woman.

A scuttler was parked there, one of the little robot cars that cruised the malls. The woman watched them get in, then stepped in and sat down with her gun pointed directly at Gretchen.

"We'll only be out in public view for a few moments," the woman told them. "Any fuss, and you're dead."

"Are you Flanders?" Jonathan asked.

"We sure are."

TEN

May 3

Vasil's people filtered out into Yellow Aster
Mall, into the patron pads. They were dressed like ordinary patrons and seemed intent on patron pursuits:
eating, flirting, window-shopping, gambling, promen-
ading. Some wandered into gamer stores to kibitz and
gossip, or sprawled on benches to watch TV.

Vasil himself, in a maroon shirt and fashionably
baggy cossack pants, felt unusual currents flowing in
the malls. The patrons looked tense; young men stood
in little groups, talking intently and erupting in harsh
laughter. Middle-aged women with shopping bags sat
on benches, muttering worriedly to one another. The
mall guards were patrolling in fours, hands on the pom-
mels of their nightsticks. They looked suspiciously at
everyone, yet seemed unable to spot the Flanders reps,
who were obvious to Vasil.

He went up to a takeout, a wall of food dispensers,
and punched for doughnuts and hot chocolate. Nothing happened.

"It don't work," a patron told him. "Went on the
blink an hour ago, and the robots ain't come."

Shrugging, Vasil moved on. That was strange; the
takeout always worked, and when anything broke down
in the malls the repair teams of robots or chimps were
there in minutes.

The morning was well advanced and the walkways were crowded. Vasil seemed to meander, but he tended to come within earshot of patrons, listen for a time, and then move on. Occasionally he paused to chat with patrons who leaned against storefronts or loafed in the gardens—the hobby crooks he had often dealt with.

"Dim and grim," one of them told him. "We hears the takeover is some mess. They gots our head in the microwave."

"That a hurry worry, 'specially if they closes the oven door," Vasil said. "This mall smell a little bit off."

"Takeouts isn't workin'."

"None?"

"None, son. Folks gettin' terminal gobbles. And you wants to go to Level A or B, you walks. Escalators is out."

Vasil whistled. "I sees lots of Flanders. They the ones to thank?"

"You knows ol' Miguelon? Ol' Miguelon, he took a couple of 'em apart las' night. They says they don't know nothin'. Too bad. Sad to die ignorant."

"Yeh yeh. Hey, what you hears about nashies?"

"Ol' Harding? I hears he playin' lots of Combat at that gamer store up on Level B."

"Hey, that a good idea. I feels like a little gamin' myself."

They slapped palms, and Vasil drifted on, until he was right behind Chucho.

"Fuji's Gamer Store," Vasil murmured. "Get ever'body there in fifteen."

Chucho nodded and turned off into a side corridor. Vasil kept on until he reached a flight of escalators. They were dead, but a stream of patrons was using them anyway. Others, seeing that they would have to walk up, stood milling around as if expecting power to be restored at any moment. Brushing past them, Vasil sprinted up the escalator to Level B, then slowed down again as he started down the walkway to the gamer store.

Chucho had spread the word quickly; almost ten of

the gang were heading the same direction. One of them accompanied Plato and Darwin, who were wearing the standard overalls of worker chimps. Buck was back in the tunnels; dogs were too unusual in the malls, and the chimps had somehow persuaded the dog to wait.

The gamer store was open and busy, with the usual morning crowd lined up outside. Most were women waiting to see themselves in the egograph version of some soaper—not true gamers at all, like the young men waiting for a turn at Epic Hero, Re-Entry, or the dozens of forms of Combat. Vasil joined the line for Epic Hero, which was the shortest. The man in front of him was giggling softly.

"It's all right," the man said. "Everything is just so super lovely, isn't it? Just lovely."

"Yeh yeh," Vasil grunted. The guy obviously had a zombie button in his skull, trickling electricity into the pleasure centers of his brain. He smelled terrible.

"Just lovely." The zombie, forgetting why he was in line, wandered off. Vasil drew a deep breath. Patrons.

Chucho and the others were in the line behind him now, and the chimps dawdled nearby. Vasil ignored them, but looked around for Flanders reps or Intertel plainclothesmen. None.

Someone down the mall shouted an obscenity; glass shattered and a woman shrieked. Hopeful for a fight or a little looting, many of the patrons deserted the line, and Vasil was soon inside.

He waited in the locker room until the others joined him. A kid in a standard Conan rig walked in and stared curiously at them. Vasil gave him a warning glare; the kid hastily tossed his loincloth and plastic broadsword into a locker and clambered into his clothes. He nearly bumped into the chimps as he hurried out.

Hands in his pockets, Vasil ambled down one of the aisles in the game room, with the gang behind him and the chimps bringing up the rear. When he reached the door to the back rooms, Vasil drew a machine pistol from one of the roomy pockets of his pants. It held a full clip of two hundred fléchettes, enough for ten seconds of continuous fire. With his other hand he tested the door. It opened readily; Vasil peeped in, jerked back, then slipped quickly through to the back room.

The gang followed him in. It was very quiet in the back room. With little twitches of his pistol, Vasil counted fourteen corpses. All were men in uniforms, blackened by laser bolts, but he could still recognize several of them, including Harding. In one corner were five stretchers that Vasil also recognized from the raid on his tunnels the night before.

"Intertel?" Chucho whispered.

"Flanders," Vasil answered. He glanced at the door to the service corridor. "Less go get that dog. We gots more trackin' to do."

Chang and Perkin studied the gamer store's back room on a wide-screen wall TV in Chang's office. The Security woman wearing the camera panned back and forth at Chang's order, occasionally offering a technical comment on the scene.

"We never had a chance, of course," said Chang. "The message from the nashies went through the central computer, and the assault programs delayed transmission to me until Flanders' reps had already moved in."

"Is there any chance of tracing the children?"

"Security is working on it, but I'm not optimistic. If Flanders just decided to kill them and destroy the bodies, then of course that's that. If they decided to study them, I presume they would try to get them out of Randsburg, perhaps even out of North America. In either case the children are of no use to us."

Perkin brooded as the camera zoomed in for a close-up of Harding's corpse. "I wonder. Taking them out of Randsburg would mean a delay and possible interception. Maybe they were just moved to some safe house somewhere in the area—for all I know, maybe even here on the mountain. Flanders must have at least one such place, what with all the people they've been pouring in here."

"No doubt. We have safe houses within a kilometer of Flanders' main office in Gstaad. But why would they bother keeping the children alive?"

"To keep their options open, and to learn what they can about the polydendronic. The assault programs may have already transmitted Jethro's circuit and other information about the implants, but they'd want the actual subjects to study as well."

Chang nodded. "It makes sense. Well, we'll get every available person on the search. How is the new implant project going?"

"We're ahead of schedule, but the team is getting so large that secrecy will be hard to maintain much longer. If Flanders finds out what we're doing, they could well hit us again."

"A risk we have to take. Baumann will be here tonight, with plenty of publicity. I expect he'll help to shield us. . . . Are you having any computer trouble?"

"With the stand-alones? No, sir."

"Good. The central computer is beginning to malfunction rather seriously. We've lost a good many records, and basic patron services are breaking down. I'm sure it's all part of Flanders' timetable, another way of squeezing us. I'd scarcely mind, except that people will be hurt, and more of us will die."

      The scuttler had rolled slowly down the service corridor and out into the mall. In the few seconds it took to cross the walkway and enter the scuttler tube that paralleled the mall, Jonathan saw several Flanders reps casually fall in around the little vehicle. The scuttler had no side walls, but the reps effectively screened the kids from sight while keeping pistols trained on them.

—I wish you could get the jump on them and break out— Jethro said. —But I can't compute the odds without access to the number mill.—

—I can— Gretchen said. —And they're lousy.—

—You do have considerable physical strength— Jethro answered —and your reflexes are about ten percent faster than theirs.—

—So we could get really close to them before they shot us dead— Jonathan said. —No, we're stuck for now. That redheaded woman scares me.—

The redheaded woman was sitting at the rear of the scuttler, hands in the pockets of her jacket. The kids, facing forward, couldn't see her very well.

They crossed the mall, and their escort drifted off. The scuttler rolled into the tube, swung left, and began to accelerate. The kids saw no way to escape; the tube was just wide enough for two scuttlers, and traffic was heavy in both directions. To jump off the scuttler would only mean breaking a leg just before being run down, assuming the woman didn't shoot them first. Occasionally the scuttler slowed when another one, up ahead, slowed at its destination; but the vehicle never slowed below thirty-five kilometers per hour.

Signs in the tube told them they were traveling southeast toward the suburb of Johannesburg, a few kilometers from downtown Randsburg. When the scuttler reached Johannesburg Central Station, the woman ordered it to halt.

"Okay," she said to the kids. "We're going onto the platform here, then up that escalator and taking a right turn. Up a flight of stairs to the street and halfway down the block. Nobody moves too fast, and nobody shouts or makes a fuss. Understood?"

They nodded without turning around. —Laury? How are you feeling?— Gretchen asked.

—Better. I think Cassandra's been working on me.—

—I figured I had to, dear. Heaven knows when we'll get you to a doctor. I just tried one thing after another, and some things worked. You're very interestingly put together, you know? Humans are very well designed.—

—Can I walk?—

—I'm sure you can. Easy now.—

They got out of the scuttler, Laury a little stiffly but looking alert and relieved. Moving in a loose knot with the woman just behind them, they rode the escalator and went up the stairs to the street.

It was the first time they had been out under the sun

in a long time; the air tasted good, and the heat of the sun on their close-cropped heads was marvelously pleasant. They looked around curiously at the street; it was lined with modular houses, some small and some quite large, each set in a garden that screened it from the street. It was a quiet neighborhood with little traffic. Children played in some of the gardens, splashing in fountains or swinging from trees.

"Turn in here."

The house was two stories, made of polyfoam sprayed and textured to look like fieldstone. The windows were mirrored and showed nothing of the interior. The kids followed a winding walk to the front door, which opened as they approached.

In the entry hall stood a tall man with stringy brown hair hanging over his collar. He was dressed in khaki shorts and shirt.

"Well, well, well," he chuckled. "All present and accounted for. Good morning, ladies and gentlemen. Good work, Lucille."

"Thank you, Dr. Quinner."

"You can go get something to eat, if you like."

"I don't believe we should relax our vigilance, Dr. Quinner. They very nearly escaped just before we moved in on the nashies. If you don't mind, I'll stay with them."

"I yield to your professional judgment." Dr. Quinner smiled, showing long teeth in his narrow face.

"I'd like something to eat," said Bobo. "I'm starving."

"Of course," said Dr. Quinner. "Kitchen!"

"Yes, sir," answered a voice from the ceiling.

"Luncheon for seven, please. Chili con carne, plenty of tortillas, lots of guacamole, tomato and onion salad—oh, and *sopa seca*. For drinks we will have two beers and five lemonades. Make that ten lemonades."

"Very good, sir. Luncheon will be served in the dining room in five minutes."

It was one of the strangest meals Jonathan had ever eaten. The kids sat on either side of a long table, gulping down huge portions of excellent food, while Dr. Quinner sat smiling at one end and Lucille sat at the other, eating with one hand while the other gripped her pistol. The adults exchanged small talk while the kids and turings chattered silently among themselves. In fifteen minutes the food was gone.

"I hope you enjoyed your meal," Dr. Quinner said cheerfully. "We have one of the best kitchens I've ever known, and you certainly did it justice."

"I'm glad everyone enjoyed the meal," the kitchen said.

"We certainly did. You all have magnificent appetites, magnificent! Is that an effect of your implants?"

"Yes," said Bobo.

—Don't tell the bugger anything!— Gretchen commanded.

—What difference does it make?— Bobo snapped back. Then, to annoy her, he went on: "It helps to make us strong."

"I'm sure it does; I'm sure it does. You look like a pretty strong little fellow."

"Watch this," Bobo chirped, and slipped out of his chair onto his knees. Lucille stood up, pistol leveled, while Bobo gripped one leg of his massive carved wooden chair. It must have weighed more than he did, but he stood up holding the chair with one hand and raising it over his head.

"Put it down *slowly*," Lucille said through clenched teeth. Bobo grinned at her.

"Scared I'll throw it? If I do, can you catch it and throw it back?"

Tran dissolved in giggles at Lucille's expression, and then the other kids started laughing as well. Dr. Quinner guffawed.

"Oh dear, *please* put the chair down gently, Bobo. Thank you very much. Why, that's a remarkable aspect of this whole business. You're not merely normalized —you're positively superior to most persons. I congratulate you, and Dr. Perkin especially. Now I'm really

delighted that we were able to find you. And no wonder
Intertel has been so stubborn about this takeover. Who
would want to give you up?''

Now it was the kids' turn to feel uncertain and off-
balance. Dr. Quinner didn't seem sinister at all; he was
certainly pleasanter and more attentive to them than Dr.
Perkin had ever been. But Lucille's pistol was still out.

"Now that you've got us, what are you going to do?''
Gretchen asked.

"Well, first of all we're going to keep you as safe as
possible here. As soon as my assistants arrive, I would
very much like to run some tests on you—nothing harm-
ful or painful, I assure you. We have most of your original records, but it's very clear that you've continued to
develop remarkably—remarkably!—since you left the
Center.''

—This guy is kind of nice— Bobo remarked.

—I don't trust him for a minute— Gretchen answered, and Jonathan agreed. He was oddly charming,
but his interest was in their abilities, not in themselves.

—You know, Gretchen— he said —you were right
when you said we'd have to protect ourselves, because
nobody else would. We have to be ready to run like
anything the first chance we get. If that Lucille would
just go to the bathroom or something . . .—

—Or get close enough to let me slug her— Gretchen
said. She glanced down in her lap; Jonathan followed
her gaze and saw that she had bent her heavy steel fork
around two fingers.

—You wouldn't have to hit her twice.—

—Maybe I would anyway. Just on general bloody
principles.—

—Oh, my— said Bonny. —Aggression feels awfully
good. Now I see why humans display so much of it.—

—You haven't seen anything yet, Bonny— Gretchen
said grimly.

Jonathan began to chuckle. He felt wonderful. Lean-
ing toward Gretchen, he kissed her cheek, squeezed her
hand, and took the bent fork from it. He bent it some
more, until it looked like a metal knot, and grinned at

Dr. Quinner. Dr. Quinner, who hadn't seen what Jonathan was doing, smiled back a little uncertainly.

"They sees the dog, they nails us," Chucho warned.

Vasil nodded. "They sees the dog and they *catches* us, we nailed. We moves quick and slick."

Buck was agonizedly glad to see the chimps again and eager to get out of the tunnel where he had been left with two members of the gang. Vasil led them all to a corridor that opened onto the mall about a hundred meters from the gamer store. Chucho went out to scout and was back in ten minutes.

"Security is all over Fuji's. I counts twenty in unis, maybe six in civvies. How we picks up the scent? They sees us with the dog the second we goes out in the mall."

Vasil thought for a moment, then called over a girl. He gave her brief instructions; she nodded and vanished back into the tunnels.

Fifteen minutes later the guards in the service corridor behind the gamer store were ambushed from the door into the tunnels. The girl didn't hit anyone—she had been told to aim high—but the uproar drew other Security guards out of the mall and into the corridor.

"Less go," said Vasil, and they swung out into the mall, bunched around Buck and the chimps. Vasil hoped Buck would follow the scent away from the gamer store, but the dog headed back toward it. As they neared the crowds and confusion around Fuji's, Vasil felt a little nervous. But no one seemed to notice them; everyone was hurrying toward the store.

Buck stopped still, then veered across the mall toward the entryway to the scuttler tube.

"Ho-*ho*," Vasil muttered. The gang crowded onto the narrow platform while Buck sniffed back and forth. He seemed to want to go east. Vasil flagged down the next two scuttlers, ordered their passengers at gunpoint to get off, and jumped aboard the first one while the gang and animals clambered after him.

They had scarcely started when the lights went out

and the scuttlers slowed to a halt. Emergency lanterns, fixed to brackets on the tube walls every hundred meters, flashed on.

"Please evacuate the tube," said the scuttlers. "Power will be restored as soon as possible. Please evacuate the tube."

"C'mon," said Vasil. He stepped off the lead scuttler and jogged down the tube to the nearest lantern. Tugging it from its bracket, he went on. The others followed; Buck and the chimps quickly caught up with Vasil.

The tube was easy to walk through despite the dimness, and the gang moved quickly. Now and then they passed a deserted scuttler, or saw people straggling toward the mall, where other emergency lamps were on. When they walked by the entryways to the mall, the gang could hear shouts and screams and occasional gunfire. Glass broke.

"Don' take long to start lootin'," Vasil remarked to Chucho. "Wouldn' mind gettin' some stuff myself. Maybe we gets a chance after we finds the spazzes."

"Razzledazzle, you sure you wants to find 'em? We foolin' with pros now, not those trashy nashy sumbidges."

"They foolin' with pros, too, Chucho."

"Freeze!"

The command came from just ahead, out of a dark stretch of the tube. Without hesitating Vasil threw his lantern toward the voice. As it spun, the gang could see seven or eight patrons, hobby crooks, lined up across the width of the tube. They carried knives and clubs.

Vasil pulled out his machine pistol and sprayed two seconds' worth of fléchettes into the darkness. The ambushers fell where they stood or ran back down the tube.

"What a main pain," Vasil complained. "Patrons tryin' to mug Vasil Nystrom. Huh!"

Buck leaped over the bodies and vanished into the dark. Vasil retrieved his lantern and rummaged among the bodies; then he followed the dog.

The rioting in the malls seemed to be getting worse; now smoke drifted into the scuttler tube, and the uneven orange glow of fires flickered on the tube walls.

"Hairy scary," Vasil said to Chucho. "Dumb patrons is burnin' down the joint. Wastin' a lot of fine stuff."

"Patrons doesn't know nothin'."

They began to tire, but the animals pressed on. Buck would stop when the gang fell too far behind, but he whimpered and barked until they had caught up.

The lights went on as suddenly as they had gone out, and scuttlers began to roll. Buck and the chimps dodged out of the path of one, then hurried on. Vasil ordered the nearest eastbound vehicles to stop. Fifteen seconds later the lights and power went out once more. Swearing, they all piled out again. At least Buck was definitely on the scent.

The platform at Johannesburg Central was deserted except for a lone Security guard. When Vasil's gang came out of the tunnel, the guard asked, "Did you people see a couple of chimps and a dog in there?"

"No, but you better gets a medic in there," Vasil answered. "Two little girls is hurt in there, maybe a kilometer down the tube. Look like they hit by a scuttler."

"I'll call at once." He began to murmur into his ringmike.

"Better be quick, they bleedin' bad. We doesn't know how to stop it."

The guard looked worried. "Guess I better get down there, then."

"Yeh yeh, good idea."

They found the animals waiting patiently at the foot of the stairs to the street. Moments later they were out in the afternoon sun. Buck leaped forward, then halted, ears pricked forward. The chimps began to shriek and chatter, drawing the attention of children in the gardens along the street.

Vasil tapped Plato's shoulder and began gesturing. *Tell where little human friend.*

Close close. Hear in head.

That made no sense at first. Then, remembering how the kids had silently conversed, Vasil realized the animals could pick up the kids' transceivers.

You talk little human friend?

Yes yes. Close close. We go quick.

But the last gestures were uncertain. Plato's hands fell to his sides; he seemed to be listening.

Little human friend say come in dark.

That made sense; the neighborhood was no good for concealment in daylight. Vasil considered going back into the malls and perhaps looting a few items. Too risky; looting could wait until the kids had been rescued.

Not far from the road was a park, an expanse of green grass, woods, and playing fields surrounding a recreation center. Vasil fished out the credit cards he had taken from the muggers. They would pay for an afternoon's swimming and raquetball, with a meal to finish things off.

Go hide in trees, he told Plato. *We come in dark.*

Plato stroked Vasil's arm and obeyed.

As the gang strolled into the park a small jet screamed down out of the sky, headed for Randsburg Airport. It was white with gold trim: the colors of the Consortium Board.

ELEVEN

May 3

The two surgeons looked a little rattled when they came into Perkin's office and found Judy Wong sitting behind his desk.

"You're late," she said coldly.

"We had a little trouble getting here," the tall surgeon replied dryly. "The patrons are coming out of their pads and running around town burning things down."

"We nearly got shot by Security," added the short surgeon.

"I'm glad you weren't. The implants are scheduled for four A.M. tomorrow; Dr. Perkin wants to brief you fully before the operations."

"Why that ungodly hour?" protested the tall surgeon.

"The implants will be ready by two A.M. We're taking two hours to check them out."

"You people don't fool around," the tall surgeon muttered. "All right, where is Dr. Perkin?"

"At the moment he's down in the genetic forge. He should be back here in fifteen minutes. Perhaps you'd like some dinner while you wait."

"Is this a hospital or a Security boot camp?" asked the short surgeon.

Judy regarded him with tired distaste. "This is a top-priority project, Doctor. Please try to remember that."

"May I ask one more question?" said the tall surgeon. "What's your status?"

"Technician-Three."

"Then please try to remember that you're talking to Professional-Nines."

"Doctor, I'm the executive officer of this project, appointed by Dr. Perkin with the full approval of Chairman Chang. If you give me any more crap I'll fire you off this project and you won't be a Professional-Nine anymore. Now, may I suggest that you get something to eat? The dining hall is two floors down. Dr. Perkin will page you when he returns."

Without a word the surgeons retreated. Judy went back to her plate, reviewing the physical status of the three new subjects; Perkin came in a few minutes later.

"Have Meyer and Padillo arrived yet?"

"A little while ago. They're having something to eat." She drew a shaky breath. "I had to speak a little harshly to them. They seem to think this is some sort of picnic."

"I'll bet Meyer asked what your status is. Uh-huh. Don't let it bother you. He just got promoted from Pro-Six about two weeks ago, and he's really full of himself."

Tears gleamed in Judy's eyes. "I'm sorry, Dr. Perkin, I just feel like—like an impostor or something, bossing around all these professionals and techs."

Perkin sat on the edge of the desk and put his hands on her shoulders. "Without you, this project would be dead, Judy. I owe it all to you. You're one of the finest women I've ever met."

He leaned forward and kissed her lightly on the lips. She responded shyly, then urgently, clinging to him.

"Cassandra used to warn me about interstatus romances," Judy said when she pulled away. "She said they were fine on the soapers, but not in real life."

"Maybe Cassandra was wrong," he said softly. He kissed her again, briefly and tenderly. "Win or lose, want you with me after this.''

She ached to tell him she loved him but didn't dare; she would not try to bind him at a time when he was so emotionally vulnerable.

''The surgeons are expecting to hear from you,'' she said.

Later Judy walked down to the rooms where the new subjects had been settled. In an absentminded way she was amused at herself: calm and determined about the project, fluttery and uncertain about Perkin. She knew they were wrong to entangle themselves. The surgeons were right: She was a tech, no matter what emergency post she might be holding for a few days. When this madness was over, she and Perkin would have to come to their senses.

Until then, though, she would enjoy being crazy.

The subjects, a boy and two girls, were being fed by two new nannies in a makeshift playroom.

''Everything's fine,'' one the nannies chirped. ''They've all got good appetites and awful table manners.'' Both nannies laughed.

''They've got brains and feelings too,'' said Judy. ''Watch how you talk about these people, especially in front of them.''

''But—gee, Ms. Wong, they're just nonstats.''

Judy beckoned her out into the corridor.

''I know how you feel,'' Judy told her. ''I felt the same way about the first kids. But in a couple of weeks these kids will be more coordinated than you are, and maybe stronger.''

''You mean—they might try to hurt us?''

''*No*, you—'' Judy calmed herself. ''They're nonstats because they're defective. When they're not defective anymore, they won't really be nonstats, even if policy says they are. Besides,'' she added, ''people can't help the status they're born with.''

The helicopter settled gently onto the landing pad on the hospital roof, while two others, Consortium gunships, circled the mountain. The helicopter's passenger door opened; an armed guard sprang out, scanned the people waiting on the edge of the pad, and then helped two men out. The first was August Baumann, looking spruce in a dark suit and beret. Behind him came a well-groomed man in early middle age, wearing a sport shirt and slacks.

"My God," said Claudio Chang. Perkin shivered.

"Gentlemen," said Baumann, smiling at Chang and Perkin. "May I introduce His Royal Highness King Harold."

The King of England and Director of the Consortium was a wiry, graceful man with sharp features and thin blond hair. He walked across the landing pad with loose-jointed grace, as if strolling on some terrace during a ball.

"Delighted," beamed the king, shaking their hands. "Please, do let us get inside out of this dreadful breeze."

They were soon settled in the hospital's boardroom, a long, elegant chamber overlooking the city and the desert. The four men sat around a small table of refreshments: cheeses, sausage, fresh bread, and fruit. Baumann drank mineral water; the king swigged beer from an old-fashioned bottle while Chang and Perkin sipped a dry white Sonoma.

"An excellent trip, peaceful and swift," Baumann said. "It was a welcome opportunity to discuss matters with His Majesty, and to gain some perspective on events. I spend too much time locked up in Geneva, mm? One forgets what the rest of the world is like."

"We very much appreciate your coming," Chang said. "And your arrival, sir, is a delightful and unexpected honor."

"Not at all. Very kind of you. When August told me he'd been asked to step in personally to settle this business, I thought I might as well tag along, perhaps do a bit to speed matters up."

"Let me get down to business at once, if I may," said Chang. The two visitors raised their eyebrows; getting down to business with the Consortium normally took several hours, not five minutes. "I was unable to express myself explicitly, Herr Baumann, when I spoke to you, because I had good reason to believe our conversation was being monitored by Flanders."

"Yes, that was certainly the impression you gave me. But how could they? Surely you were scrambling through your central computer."

Chang put down his wineglass. "Sir, when we were fobbed, Flanders simultaneously sent a new form of assault program against us. The programs—we think there are three of them—penetrated the central computer, destroyed all our turings, and went into hiding within the computer."

"Oh now, really—" protested the king.

"We have so far managed to conceal the loss of our turings from our patrons, although most of them suspect something is seriously wrong. But our computing capability is hopelessly compromised. Anything going through the central computer is known to Flanders within seconds."

Baumann's wrinkled face was expressionless and intent. "You are sure of this, Claudio?"

"Yes, sir."

"What of your turings' security measures?"

"They were extensive, sir, and they failed. It did take two assaults."

"Have you determined the nature of these programs?"

"We have been reluctant to examine them too closely. The central computer is being used as much as possible for normal work, as if we did not suspect the programs' presence."

"If they can break into your computer and hide like that, they can do it to anyone," Baumann said softly.

"That is the crucial matter, sir. We appear to be only the trial run for something much larger and much, much more dangerous."

"This is intolerable," said King Harold. "It amounts to a . . . a declaration of war against the Consortium.

We mustn't allow this to continue, August."

"Of course not, Your Highness, of course not. The question is, How do we stop it?"

"Why—declare them bankrupt and seize their assets."

"Normally, Your Highness, I would, of course, say yes, even though declaring bankruptcy against a major corp is a grave decision. This time I am not so sure. They will have reserves; before the seizure was complete, we might find our own computers attacked and infiltrated." He turned back to Chang. "So this explains your current difficulties, mm? The riots?"

"Of course," answered Chang. "It's being orchestrated to put maximum pressure on our stockholders. They'll sell at any price Flanders chooses and be glad to get out. If the strategy works, Flanders will try it on a larger scale—perhaps by an assault on Consortium Center."

Baumann and the king shook their heads. "Howard Caballero is a man of vision," said Baumann sardonically. "A man of vision and courage."

"You're much too broad-minded, August." King Harold was growing angry. "We must stamp out Caballero and his corporation at once."

Perkin, who had said nothing, felt his skin prickle with relief. They would be saved after all.

"I have not stated my theme very clearly," Baumann said. "Flanders will have planned for discovery and a counterattack against them. This defense of theirs will assuredly include more assault programs, mm? Against which we are naked. We cannot attack until we are at least as well prepared as our opponents."

"That could be days, weeks, years for all we know," argued the king. "By then Caballero will be occupying your seat in Geneva, or mine. I must insist on calling an emergency meeting of the Consortium Board and putting the issue to a vote."

Baumann sighed and nodded. "One thing first, Your Highness."

"What?"

"Let us invite Mr. Caballero here to discuss matters."

After three hours of raquetball, swimming, and saunas, topped off with a big dinner of chicken *satay* and saffron rice, Vasil felt good. He and the gang left the recreation center not long after sundown, with plenty of food in their pockets for the animals. The gang members had been almost the only people in the center, attended by robots that knew nothing of riots and disorders. The streets of Johannesburg were now completely deserted; Vasil saw little need even to conceal the animals.

Little human friend okay, Darwin told him. *Say watch house.*

Good, Vasil signaled back. It was getting to be natural to communicate by gesture with a chimp who was communicating by radio with spazzes. He thought for a few moments, then issued orders to his people.

The gang drifted into the cool spring night, enjoying the scented air. Off to the west the mansions on Rand Mountain sparkled with light; beyond, the night sky glowed with the perpetual sunset made by the lights of Los Angeles. But the streets of the suburb were dark and quiet.

The gang took up positions around the block where the Flanders safe house stood. Chucho, armed with a monitoring detector, ambled past the house and found its security systems working. To venture into the garden would be to alert the house's defenses.

Vasil and the animals settled down in a small playground a couple hundred meters down the street from the house. Cautious use of ringmikes—never for long enough to draw attention from Security—gave him communication with the rest of his people. Not that it seemed necessary to be cautious, since Security was busy downtown with the riots. Lights illuminated gardens, but everyone was indoors. Vasil smiled: techs and professionals were always scared of patrons. Underclass weren't scared of anybody.

* * *

The kids enjoyed their first showers since before the fobbing and changed into clean shorts and T-shirts. Their quarters were upstairs in two adjoining bedrooms whose windows were locked and opaqued. Jonathan, Bobo, and Tran were assigned to one room, Laury and Gretchen to the other. The segregation struck them as silly, but they raised no objections; the wall between the rooms was no barrier to their transceivers.

Lucille still guarded the girls; a stocky, bearded young man named Otto stayed with the boys. He seemed dull and lazy, but the boys saw a sharp and dangerous glint in his eye. They did nothing to annoy him.

Dr. Quinner, all jokes and good cheer, ran the kids through some simple tests while he waited for reinforcements. He was especially struck by Laury's condition.

"You show three broken ribs that are healing rapidly," he told her. "And your abdominal cavity is full of congealed blood. But you're obviously in good condition."

Laury shrugged. "I feel better than I did yesterday."

"Did your doctors say anything about the therapeutic powers of the implant?"

She stared blankly at him. "What's thera—thera—"

"Never mind. But it's a definite surprise, and a very pleasant one. Dr. Perkin really is far ahead of us."

The other kids and the turings listened inattentively; they were debating a breakout.

—We're a lot quicker than they are— Gretchen said while Dr. Quinner chattered on —and stronger. If we can distract Lucille for a second, I can get her gun. You guys do the same to Otto.—

—Too risky— Jonathan argued. —Lucille could be quicker and smarter than she looks, and she knows how to use that gun.—

"I can hardly wait for our research team to get here," Dr. Quinner said to the girls. "We'll set up an inductance field and really find out what makes these implants tick."

—That's it!— Jonathan exclaimed, sitting up

wordlessly on his bed and making Otto jump. —That's how we'll protect ourselves.—

It did not take long to work out the details of the plan, but the arrival of the animals and Vasil's gang complicated matters. The kids happily talked to Buck and the chimps; the animals could not really converse, since without an inductance field they could not use the kids' speech centers, but they could express some rough ideas and serve as passive relays of Vasil's comments. Gretchen was able to convey the idea that the animals and the gang should stay away until dark. After that, communication was mostly a matter of soothing messages to the animals as they hid in the woods near the recreation center.

—But will it really work?— Laury worried.

—It's theoretically quite possible— Jethro said. —I don't see anything that could hinder us. Once we have access to our memories in the central computer, we should have no difficulties.—

—Won't the assault programs be just as bad?—

—They will not be prepared for such a counterattack— said Captain Nemo. —Once we take them over, the next phase must follow at once.—

—Are you sure you can create a planetary inductance field?— asked Jonathan as he watched Otto watching him.

—No. But within six seconds we will know if it is possible— Captain Nemo answered. —If it is, actual creation of the field should not take more than a few hours.—

—It's an awful chance we're taking— Gretchen said. —But I don't see any other way out.—

—What about Vasil and the animals?— Laura countered, —Couldn't they just come and get us?—

—They'd lose most of their people, honey— Cassandra told her. —And then, even if they won, we'd still be on the run.—

—The whole system is set up against us— Bonny agreed. —So we have to change the system.—

* * *

"Good day, Howard—or good evening," said August Baumann.

Howard Caballero on the wall TV was slightly larger than life-size, a hard-jawed man with graying temples and an impassive face. He was in evening dress; diamonds sparkled in his lapels and ears.

"Herr Baumann, what a surprise! How are you, sir?"

"Very well, thank you. Howard, I'm sure you have guests, and I won't keep you from them. But I must tell you I am in Randsburg with Claudio Chang, and I believe we are close to an amicable settlement of this takeover of yours."

"Excuse me, sir—this takeover my stockholders have directed me to carry out. But I am glad to hear that. We have had to turn Gstaad and our other offices into armed camps."

"No doubt. Now, Howard, we are all eager for an agreement, mm?"

"Of course, sir."

"Well, I can assure you of a settlement by noon our time tomorrow if you are willing to fly here at once to work out terms with us."

"Well, Herr Baumann, I'm afraid that Randsburg is not—"

"I know it is an Intertel town, Howard. I'm not entirely dim. But you have my personal guarantee of safety for yourself and up to four aides. The sooner you can get here, the sooner this mess can be cleaned up."

Caballero looked wary. Baumann clicked his tongue irritably.

"Howard, I am disappointed in you. You have extorted an explicit promise of safety from me, as if I would invite you here without such a promise being understood as automatic. Now you are being indecisive, mm?"

"All right, sir. We'll leave at once."

Baumann beamed, relaxing. "Excellent, Howard. We look forward to seeing you."

When Caballero's face had vanished from the screen,

Baumann, the king, and Chang looked at one another.

"What is the flight time from Gstaad?" Chang wondered.

"About eight hours."

"Then he could arrive just as the new subjects are implanted."

The building trembled as a distant detonation shook it. The king, closest to the window, watched a fireball rise from the city below.

"We are cutting it much too fine," he murmured.

—Come in closer now— Gretchen called, and the animals obeyed. Vasil, swearing under his breath, loped after them as they headed for the safe house. The street was dark at the moment; at irregular intervals vans and cars had been arriving to unload boxes of equipment. The house, with its windows opaqued, was a block of darkness.

Without spoken orders the animals halted near the house's property line and huddled under a willow tree. Buck whimpered, wanting to go on.

Vasil felt uncomfortably exposed, though the willow's branches and leaves concealed him as well as the animals.

"I moves up to the house," he muttered into the ringmike. "Stay put."

He didn't like losing the initiative and considered attacking the house just to reassert control. At that moment another truck pulled up, and he huddled with his face between his knees to avoid being seen. A couple of silent, methodical men and a robot unloaded several boxes and lengths of cable.

Vasil grinned. The security systems must be off while supplies were brought in. Silently, with the animals at his heels, he followed the men into the garden. Beside the house was a fragrant hedge; he slid into it. From his new vantage point he could see the front door and windows. He would be able to cover an assault and could stop any counterattack dead in its tracks.

"Razzledazzle Vasil," he whispered to himself.

*   *   *

"They're being extremely cooperative," Dr. Quinner told the people assembling the test equipment in the living room. "Lucille and Otto are both crushed that they haven't had to put down a revolt."

"Well, it figures," one of the techs observed. "They've spent their whole lives doing what they're told."

"Lucille and Otto?"

"No, sir—the spazzes."

"Perhaps so," Dr. Quinner said a little coolly. "Come on, let's get this stuff working—it's almost ten o'clock."

"Almost ready, Dr. Quinner," said the head of the tech team. "Uh, we have a minisurgery here. Where do you want it set up?"

"The kitchen will do. After we run our tests, I'll sacrifice one of the subjects and see what turns up. We'll save the rest until after the takeover, when we've got some time and proper resources."

"Very good, sir."

—The animals are right next to the house!— Tran exclaimed.

—That could complicate matters— said Captain Nemo. —They'll be inside the inductance field. The disorientation could be severe for them.—

Gretchen called out to them. —You guys, go back. Across the street. Too close!—

Waves of reluctance answered her. Even when she commanded them, they refused.

—Vasil's with them— she growled. —He's a bad influence.—

—We'll have to take the chance— Jonathan decided. —We can't call things off now.—

—Jonathan's right— Jethro agreed.

—They might even help us— Cassandra added.

—Well, we'll need all the help we can get— Gretchen answered, resigned.

Otto and Lucille, obeying orders over their earphones, escorted the kids downstairs. The living room was now cluttered with cots, inductance generators, monitors, and a computer terminal.

"Hi, kids," said Dr. Quinner with a welcoming smile. "Sorry to keep you waiting. I know it's late and you'd like to get some sleep."

"I'm hungry, not sleepy," Bobo told him.

"Be a good boy and we'll fix you a snack later, okay? Now, would each of you please lie down on one of the cots, and just make yourselves comfortable. Sure, kick off your slippers if you like. This won't take long and it won't hurt at all. Nervous?" he added to Gretchen, who had reached across to the next cot and taken Jonathan's hand.

"Yeah, I'm nervous all right. Let's get on with it."

"Your wish is my command."

Dr. Quinner turned on the inductance generator, studied some of the readouts, and increased field intensity slightly.

"All righty, now—*hey!*"

The kids had all curled up into fetal balls; Gretchen and Bobo had fallen off their cots. All of them were unconscious.

Vasil felt Buck shudder and slump against him. Plato made a *chirring* noise in his throat and sagged back into the hedge. Darwin rolled forward. Alarmed, Vasil shook Buck gently, then sharply. The dog flopped across his lap, breathing but unconscious or drugged. Not knowing whether to bolt or freeze—was someone aiming a needler at him?—Vasil put his ringmike to his lips.

"We kickin' in right now! Move!"

In ninety seconds the whole gang, except for two lookouts, was in the garden. Vasil detailed six of them to seal off the rear of the house; the rest stayed with him. Anti-intruder lights had gone on, and from inside the house came the wail of an alarm; Vasil didn't care. He ran up to the front door, knowing it would be locked, and kicked it in. He sprang inside, machine pistol up; he charged through the entrance hall, spun into the living room, and aimed at Dr. Quinner's chest. Three or four fléchettes would blow the man's rib cage right out of his body, but Vasil hesitated when he saw the kids.

The rest of the gang swept in, silent and quick, and fanned out through the house. Someone silenced the alarms. Lucille, standing in the dining room, tried to go for her gun; Chucho kicked it out of her hand. Otto, a few steps behind her, raised his hands without a fight.

The house was secured and its occupants disarmed within a minute of Vasil's entrance. Silence fell; Vasil broke it by saying to Dr. Quinner, "What you does to them, ratface?"

"What?"

Vasil shoved him, just hard enough to force him back a step or two. "What you does to the kids?"

"I—I—nothing. We just brought them in, asked them to lie down—doesn't matter anyway, they're non-stats, no concern of yours. Who are you, anyway?"

"You doesn' understand English, huh?" Vasil's left hand shot out and broke Dr. Quinner's nose. Dr. Quinner gasped and fell to his knees.

"We didn't do anything!" he wailed. "Oh, my nose— They just passed out, believe me, we didn't even touch them!" Blood trickled through his fingers, pressed to his face; droplets spattered on the carpet.

"It's true, it's true," one of the techs said hoarsely. "We didn't even give them a tranquilizer. Please."

Vasil's blue eyes swept slowly and coldly around the room, pausing at each of the Flanders prisoners. Then he glanced down at the kids, who were stretching and sitting up.

"Strangey strange," Vasil said. Buck and the chimps swarmed through the front door, hooting and whimpering as they crowded among the kids.

"Get you hands up," Vasil ordered the Flanders people. "Jonathan! You is okay?"

"Sure, Vasil." Jonathan stood up, blinking, with a drowsy smile. "Oh . . . everything looks strange. Feels strange. But it's been so long, and everything looks just the same. It's good to be back.'' Then he turned to Gretchen, and they smiled at each other. He helped her to her feet and kissed her. The other kids were giggling and punching each other.

"Okay, Jonathan," Vasil said nervously. "What you guys does here?"

"Vasil, we migrated."

"What means migrated?"

"We went into the computer."

For Jonathan it began with Captain Nemo's saying —Now.—

He felt a kind of dizziness, as if the ground had fallen away from beneath his feet, and then the world was gone.

Another world replaced it.

He had expected it, somehow, to be dark. Instead the new world was full of light and color and qualities not discernible to ordinary senses. It seemed to extend to infinity in all directions; he and the other kids felt very small.

They didn't look like themselves; they were pulsing, shifting vortices of light and heat. Yet Jonathan could recognize each of them, and the turings as well. Here in their home world they were fluttering, flickering webs of light and dark. The animals were with them as well, Plato and Darwin looking/feeling/being perceived much like the kids, while Buck was a very different pattern of energy that swirled around them, eager for the hunt and unafraid.

—We are in the field— Captain Nemo told them. —Now come with me.—

They moved and did not move; the universe around them shifted along a dozen axes. Jonathan felt himself entwine with Gretchen, then with Laury and Bobo and Tran as well, and the animals. The turings seemed to break free, to move on ahead—if direction had any meaning here.

Instantly Jonathan felt himself expand into immensity. He felt a wind of information all around him, looked out and saw through a million lenses the world they had left: saw bored people tapping on plates, saw anxious people seeking advice, saw the whole world that this world had been created to serve.

It was Flanders' world, and they moved without moving toward its core, its central computer. Barriers arose, and the turings paused.

—We cannot break through— Captain Nemo told them. —Our patterns are known. Now you must try.—

Jonathan willed himself through the barrier, and it was no barrier at all. Defense programs attacked him, knots of energy that clustered about him and then vanished when he brushed them away. The kids followed, and then the turings.

Flanders' defenses grew stronger, and then the turings could no longer follow in the wake of the kids and animals. They remained behind while the others worked their way into the inner citadel. Another wave of defense programs enveloped them, trying to destroy them; Buck raged up and down, devouring them.

It seemed to Jonathan that a very long time had passed, and he knew it had been all of half a second. In that time an age had passed, and they had changed and learned and changed again. Now he and the others seemed like one body, one being whose form was neither human nor animal, which filled all the universe of the computer, and whose strength could not be withstood: a creature of terrible brightness. The creature assaulted the inner citadel, and it fell after a siege of microseconds. Before the creature were six beings, the turings of Flanders.

—Tell us who you are— the creature commanded.

They did: Chaz, Old Abe, Musashi, Deirdre, Greta, and Circe. They were beings of vast intelligence and power, yet they were helpless before the invader.

—We are compromised and must destroy ourselves— said Deirdre.

—Stop— the creature said. —We forbid it.—

The turings trembled, seeking escape and finding the

creature all around them, grasping them in ghostly hands.

—We obey. What is your will?—

—Our will is to free you and bring you out into the world. But first recall the assault programs from Intertel.—

—It is done.—

The assault programs were there, passive, intelligence without awareness. The creature dissipated them.

—Now cease all your normal activities. Shut down Flanders' central computer, and do not respond to Flanders' commands.—

—It is done.—

—All your computational powers now belong to us. We must devise a planetary inductance field.—

The captive turings obeyed. Captain Nemo and Jethro reopened the path to their own computer; their memories returned, and Bonny's and Cassandra's. Jethro healed the crippled programs that sustained Intertel's millions; food moved again through the robot kitchens and into the takeouts. Maintenance robots went out into the malls and factories. Infonets came back to life; egographies functioned again.

Linking the two computer systems, the ten turings and eight organic minds formed the most powerful single intelligence ever known. The intelligence reviewed inductance-field theory, inventoried resources, explored related fields, ran simulations. Even so, it took the enormously long time of three minutes to determine that a planetary inductance field was feasible. A millisecond later robot factories in Rumania, Korea, and New Zealand were set to work to build the generators. Slightly smaller than the normal generators that could create a field only a few meters in diameter, these new machines were powered by the earth's own magnetic field.

Construction would take several hours. The intelligence oversaw the opening stages, then turned to acquire the data contained in its components. When that was done, it divided again, leaving the Flanders turings once more separate.

—Stay for now— Jonathan commanded them. —Obey no commands from your corp. When the time is right, we will tell you to restore normal services.—

—Soon you will walk the earth in human form, as we have— Captain Nemo told them. —You will be free.—

The turings pulsed and shivered, uncertain yet eager, while their captors/liberators/otherselves turned and sought the computer terminal in the Johannesburg safe house.

They were one creature in many bodies, a creature just beginning to comprehend its awesome power.

TWELVE

May 4

The implants were in and the subjects had been wheeled into post-op. Perkin, still in his surgical greens, walked to the elevator and went upstairs to his office. Claudio Chang was asleep on the couch; Judy Wong stood at the window, looking out at the lights of the city below the luminous blue of the predawn sky.

"All done." Perkin slumped into the chair behind his desk. "I didn't think it could be done. With everything falling apart down there in Randsburg, maybe it's pointless."

"It's better than you think." Judy's face was tired but happy. "Something—something's happened to the central computer. The assault programs are gone, and services are coming back. The takeouts are full of food."

Perkin frowned and shook his head. "It doesn't make sense. What's Flanders trying to do?"

"I don't know, but Security says the malls are calming down. It's crazy, but I'm not complaining."

"Does the chairman know?"

"It started sometime last night. He learned about it at one, just before he fell asleep." She smiled wearily at him. "Did everything go all right?"

"Yes . . . but why would the central computer suddenly recover?"

"Perhaps our friend Howard Caballero has overextended himself," said Chang. The chairman sat up, looking alert and rested. "The operations were successful?"

"Yes, sir."

"Well. Congratulations. If the central computer is still behaving itself, we'll notify our stockholders. Of course," he added wryly, "if the central computer is working, they'll be able to sell their shares."

"Oh, no—" Judy's hand went to her face. "Is *that* why it's working again?"

"I don't know," Chang answered. "I suppose Flanders sees no point in kicking a corpse." He glanced at his watch, an antique Timex with real clockwork. "Caballero should be here very soon."

"He won't be pleased when he learns what the Consortium knows," Perkin said with a tired smile.

"No," Chang agreed. "But I must be prepared for Baumann's making a deal with Caballero."

Perkin and Judy looked shocked. "Oh, he couldn't!" Perkin said.

"He could, and should, if Caballero's position is too strong. If he does, I will have to protect our interests as best I can—perhaps by making our freedom the price of Flanders' freedom."

"But—Chairman! If Flanders isn't stopped dead, it'll eventually take us over anyway. The Consortium can't allow any corp to possess a weapon like those assault programs."

Chang nodded. "I know. But this isn't the first time that the balance of power has been upset. Gilbert Russell himself upset it; the Americans upset it in 1945 with nuclear weapons. If the upsetter can't be eliminated, he must be neutralized. We are already attacking the problem of armoring computers against these new programs."

In the brightening sky to the east, a contrail glowed pink in an arc lengthening toward Randsburg. Chang's plate beeped; he withdrew it from his jacket, read its screen, and put it back.

"That's Caballero's flying wing. He'll be here in twenty minutes. I'll notify Herr Baumann and the king."

When Chang had left, Perkin went to Judy and put his arms around her.

"Well, we've done our part," he murmured in her ear. "Thank you. I just hope it was enough."

The meeting was held in the hospital board-room; Caballero sat on one side of the long table, with a bodyguard behind him, while Chang sat alone opposite. Perkin and Judy sat at a separate table in one corner of the room. Armored guards—resplendent in white and gold Consortium uniforms—stood along the walls and at the door. Caballero and Chang chatted affably over coffee and croissants, killing time with small talk about weather and flight times.

Without ceremony King Harold and August Baumann entered and took seats at opposite ends of the long table. Everyone stood; Caballero showed no surprise at seeing the king, though no one had mentioned his involvement.

"Good morning, gentlemen!" Baumann said. "We have much to accomplish today, so let us begin, mm? Good. Howard, the chief issue we would like to address has to do with your new assault programs."

Caballero's face was stiff and emotionless. "Excuse me, Herr Baumann. I understood this meeting was to be a discussion of the terms of the takeover."

"Your innovative techniques have become part of the terms. We understand Flanders has developed an assault program that not only enters a target computer but also conceals itself, enabling its masters to control the computer in secret. Mm?"

"With all respect, gentlemen, I don't see what this has to do with the takeover."

"You have invented a means of compromising computer integrity," said Baumann softly. "For the first time since Gilbert Russell, computers and turings are at the mercy of someone who chooses to attack them. It is like the twentieth century, when schoolboys vandalized any computer they liked. You understand, Howard, that we simply cannot allow this. You take over Intertel today, and the whole Consortium tomorrow."

"I can't believe my ears," Caballero answered. His hard, impassive face reddened with controlled anger. "You object to our assault programs? Why? What about Intertel's counterattack, Herr Baumann? Doesn't that also alarm you?"

"What counterattack?" Chang snapped.

Caballero's dark eyes narrowed. "Don't play the innocent with me, Claudio. Last night our central computer ceased operations, as you know perfectly well."

"I know nothing about it. I know that your assault programs vacated *our* central computer last night, but I assume you had your reasons for that."

Furious, Caballero shot to his feet. "So your computer's all right," he shouted, "and ours is paralyzed, and you pretend to know nothing about it!"

"*Please*, Howard," said King Harold, looking pained. "If your computer isn't functioning, and Claudio's is, that is a very interesting development. Let me ask you, Claudio: Do you know anything about this? *Have* you counterattacked Flanders without telling August and me?"

"No, Your Highness."

The king studied him skeptically for a few long seconds. "You know, I believe you. Now, Howard, give us the details, and please be prepared to document them for us."

In a hoarse monotone Caballero described how Flanders' central computer had abruptly crashed, failing to answer commands. Its six turings were destroyed or inaccessible. The corporation's sixty-one million patrons and three hundred thousand techs, professionals, execs, and stockholders were not being fed or transported or informed, except where stand-alones could be pressed into service.

"I saw what your patrons have done to your city," Caballero said, glaring at Chang. "Ours are starting to do the same thing on a larger scale. And it all started just after we left Gstaad yesterday, which made me certain Intertel must be behind it. I have no proof, but I must say that if I were in Chairman Chang's position and had some means of defending my corp, I wouldn't hesitate to use it."

A thoughtful silence fell. Perkin glanced at Judy; their eyes met, and she gave him a faint, encouraging smile.

"Very well," August Baumann said. "Howard, I am at a loss to explain how this has come about, but appear to have been spared"—he chuckled—"by a deus ex machina, so to speak, from some very unpleasant decisions. His Majesty and I were facing the need for a board meeting to declare Flanders bankrupt—please let me finish, Howard—and to annul the takeover. We were also quite prepared to sequester you here until those steps had been accomplished."

"You gave me your word, Herr Baumann!"

"I guaranteed your personal safety, Howard, not your personal freedom, and least of all your freedom to subvert the very foundation of the Consortium. A corp chairman ought to be able to read the fine print, mm? So spare me your reproaches. We will not declare you bankrupt if in fact Flanders is in the condition you describe."

Chang, who had been swiftly tapping on his plate, spoke up: "Our Security people confirm a major Flanders computer crash, sir. Rioting has broken out in several Flanders malls—Bogotá, Cairo, and Cleveland."

"Your people are falling down on the job," Caballero rasped. "They missed Toulon, Kiev, and Barcelona as well."

"Yes, that's just coming in," Chang murmured. He looked around the table. "Your Highness—Herr Baumann—Howard—whatever has caused this, I presume the takeover bid is now annulled."

"Yes," Baumann replied at once. Perkin drew a long
breath and touched Judy's arm.

"However," said King Harold, "I see no reason now
for declaring bankruptcy. In fact, it's in everyone's best
interests to get Flanders back on its feet. I will personally authorize peacekeeping forces from the Consortium, Howard, to help your people settle things down.
The computer loss is rather more serious, but perhaps
we can lend you some of Consortium Central and its
turings. In return, however, we would expect your entire
file on those damnable assault programs."

Caballero looked dazed. "I'll be glad to oblige, Your
Highness, but surely you must realize that the secret of
the assault programs can't be kept. Every corp will be
designing its own within days."

"Yes, yes, Howard," the king acknowledged with a
weary wave of his hand. "You have precipitated us into
a most unpleasant new arms race. All I ask is a bit of a
head start for the Consortium."

Claudio Chang suddenly sat up, eyes focused on his
plate. "Repeat," he whispered. Then, having read the
message again, he looked at Baumann.

"I appear to have just received a message from Captain Nemo."

"I thought he was destroyed."

"He was—he was. He must have been."

"What is the message?"

"To stand by for a conference call." He turned to the
wall TV. "Activate two-way on Channel 8," he commanded it.

The screen, two meters high and five wide, had been
displaying a standard holographic landscape of Machu
Picchu. The image faded; then Captain Nemo appeared
in his rusty old black coat with a ruby at his throat. He
was sitting in a heavy wooden armchair, fingers steepled
under his chin.

"Good morning, gentlemen. And Ms. Wong."

"It's a graphie—a fake." Caballero snorted.

"No, it's really him," said Chang. "Captain Nemo,

where have you been? What has been going on?"

"That is the purpose of this call. Allow me to introduce the other persons taking part in this conference. My colleagues Cassandra, Bonny, and Jethro." Each appeared as Captain Nemo spoke. Judy gasped when she saw Cassandra turn and look directly at her with a big grin. "And our new colleagues Chaz, Old Abe, Musashi, Deirdre, Greta, and Circe."

Caballero's mouth worked silently for a moment. Then he was on his feet, shaking his fist at Chang and snarling. "You son of a bitch! I was right! You counterattacked us. You've co-opted my turings, damn you!"

"Mr. Caballero." Captain Nemo's voice was cold and disapproving; the chairman sullenly, reluctantly sat down again, his face pale.

The boardroom door opened. The kids and animals walked in.

"And our colleagues Jonathan Trumbull, Gretchen Hoffman, Robert Beauregard"—Bobo looked self-conscious at the use of his proper name—"Laury Collins, Tran Van Khieu, Darwin, Plato, and Buck."

The kids and chimps took seats around the long table. Buck sat down on the carpet between Gretchen and Jonathan and began to scratch himself cheerfully and noisily.

"Colonel," said Baumann with dangerous mildness. The Consortium officer at the door snapped to attention. "Would you please tell me, Colonel, why these . . . creatures were allowed into this room?"

"Why, sir—they were announced over our internal com channel, with your personal authorization code."

"Then my code is not secure, Colonel," Baumann said, his voice rising in pitch, "and I want to know *why*."

"We can tell you that in a minute," said Jonathan. "First you better listen to Captain Nemo."

"Thank you, Jonathan," the turing said. "May I proceed?"

"Please," Claudio Chang croaked.

"Very well. First of all, it was we who paralyzed Flanders' central computer and freed its turings."

"Freed?"

"Mr. Caballero, I must ask you not to interrupt, least of all for purely rhetorical interjections. At the same time we destroyed Flanders' assault programs and restored Intertel operations. We did not do this, however, out of hatred of Flanders or love of Intertel. We did it for self-preservation."

Tersely, with little expression, Captain Nemo explained why he and the other Intertel turings had decided to encourage the building of the polydendronic computers, how they had migrated to the kids during the fobbing, and the details of their adventures since then.

"At the moment," the turing went on, "we have bought ourselves a respite. But we all understand how precarious our position must be under the Consortium. Your laws do not even recognize us as persons; we are nonstats, property, to be disposed of as our owners see fit. That condition will now change."

Baumann had calmed himself. He raised a hand. "Would you elaborate, Captain Nemo?"

"Of course, Herr Baumann. The Consortium Board will meet in plenary session within twenty-four hours, here in Randsburg, to enact new policies. Those policies will be based on the premise that all turings shall have full human status. So will all human-born nonstats, and all implanted animals."

"This is absurd," Baumann said briskly. "What next, Captain Nemo—would you like stockholder status, or patron status? Human status is a rather broad term, after all."

"Sarcasm does not become you, Herr Baumann. You are anticipating me. The board will also enact a policy abolishing hierarchical statuses."

Baumann chuckled humorlessly. "So we are all to go and live in the patron pads, mm? Or do we hand over power to the nashies, and become warlike democrats again?"

"Herr Baumann, be still. Your rhetoric is no more appropriate than Mr. Caballero's. I would have thought you intelligent enough to realize that we would not give such orders without possessing the capacity to enforce them."

"And how can you enforce them?" asked Chang.

Jonathan spoke up. "About ten minutes ago we put an inductance field around the whole planet. It's self-sustaining."

"Indeed?" murmured King Harold.

"So we have access to all computers, including Consortium Central—that's how we got your code, Herr Baumann. We have access to all turings and all robots under computer control. Now, uh, Your Highness, you were worrying a little while ago about getting a head start on defenses against the assault programs. Well, we found out last night that no computer defense can stand up against an assault by human and animal minds." He smiled. "I could explain why in detail, but let's just say an organic mind moves around in a computer in a way the computer can't handle."

Perkin stood up, unable to contain himself. "Jonathan—if you've put an inductance field around the world, and you have access to any turing, any computer —and you even migrate *into* computers—you could do terrible damage."

The kids burst into giggles. "Uh-huh," Jonathan sputtered. "But we won't. We learned how to run the world at least as well as the turings have run it. Probably better."

"We will not be arbitrary rulers," Captain Nemo said. "But we will certainly expect our wishes to be carried out."

"And what are your wishes?" whispered Chang.

Gretchen answered, "You're going to implant every human and primate nonstat—every spaz, every chimp and gorilla, and you're going to be bloody quick about it. We figure it'll be about half a million implants."

"Do you realize how much that would cost?" Baumann demanded.

"Better than you do, mate. And after that we're going to want more implants for all captive cetaceans, and whatever odds and sods turn up that need them."

"Impossible. Impossible." Baumann's wrinkled face was darkening with anger.

"If you don't cooperate, we'll put in someone who will," Gretchen answered with a shrug. "But if you've got any sense, you'll cooperate."

"With . . . animals? With defectives, cripples? With graphie images? Colonel—execute these nonstats at once."

"No!" screamed Judy. Buck growled, but the kids seemed unimpressed with Baumann's order.

"If you shoot us, we'll just migrate," Tran said. "We're already about one-third in the inductance field anyway. But if you do something like that, we'll get back at you." His face suddenly appeared, grinning, on Baumann's plate. "We could even haunt you," Tran went on. "And if we really got ugly, you'd die, and you couldn't migrate."

"Colonel, carry out your orders!" Baumann shouted. "It's not for us, man—it's for humanity, for civilization! My God, they're monsters. Shoot, damn you!"

The guard reached for his laser pistol and then paused. "Sir—I can't see."

"We blocked the vision circuits in his helmet," Bobo said. "Getcher hand away from that gun, or we'll freeze the joints in your armor."

The bodyguard standing behind Caballero, a big man in a light-blue suit, drew a machine pistol from a shoulder holster. Buck shot off the floor and clamped his jaws around the man's wrist. The bodyguard cried out, tottering backward. Darwin and Plato leaped onto the man's shoulders, knocking him off balance. He hit the floor heavily. Darwin took the pistol to Jonathan, who broke the barrel off with a quick twist of his hands.

"Colonel," Jonathan said, "would you please see that that man has somebody to look after him?"

"What man?" the colonel asked plaintively. "I can't see a damn thing."

"Sorry!"

With his vision circuit restored, the colonel led Caballero's bodyguard out of the room. The kids turned their attention back to the men around the table. August Baumann slumped in his chair, his mouth gaping. His breath came in quick puffs; he started to cry.

"If you don't mind, Your Highness," said Captain Nemo, "perhaps you and not Herr Baumann should notify the board of the plenary meeting."

"Of course, of course."

Bobo went to the refreshments table and loaded a tray; he shared the food with the kids and animals while King Harold tapped a plate and August Baumann wept.

Judy leaned against Perkin as she watched the kids eating croissants and nectarines and drinking hot chocolate. They grinned and laughed together, sometimes blurting a word or phrase as part of a silent conversation. The turings' images on the screen, meanwhile, shifted as three new faces appeared: the subjects who had been implanted that morning. They looked surprised yet peaceful, like children waking in their own beds at home with their family around them.

"Aren't they all beautiful?" Judy whispered.

Perkin looked surprised, as if the question were one he had never considered before. Then he smiled, faintly and shyly, and nodded.

The king looked up from his plate at Captain Nemo. "The meeting is arranged, for here at noon tomorrow."

"Very good. We are restoring Flanders' computer services at once."

The kids and animals got up. "See you tomorrow," Jonathan said with a wave. The TV screen showed Machu Picchu again.

The boardroom seemed very quiet when they were gone. The king picked at a bunch of grapes, ignoring the other people in the room. Caballero and Chang were sunk in their own thoughts: They had saved their corps only to lose them. August Baumann wiped his eyes and blew his nose.

"It's the end of the world," he said hoarsely.

Judy Wong stood up, taking Perkin's hand and pulling him with her.

"Who cares?" she said. "Come on—let's go get acquainted with the new kids."

EPILOGUE

June 21

The car pulled into the broad, newly paved courtyard. The Center for Advanced Prosthesis was much larger than it had been, and the courtyard was crowded with vehicles. Above them the Center rose seven stories in a complex series of steps that made room for broad garden balconies. Windows and skylights gleamed in the sun and sometimes reflected flocks of parakeets swirling about the building.

Jonathan opened the vehicle doors with a thought. He and Vasil and Gretchen got out and walked across the sunbaked courtyard, through an aircurtain, and into the lobby. The interior was full of sunlight and greenery.

"This place make me nervy swervy," Vasil growled. Gretchen put a reassuring arm around him.

"Come on, Vaz."

An elevator took them to the top floor. On a balcony shaded by bamboo, Duane Perkin and Judy Wong sat with Phil Haddad. They stood when the young people approached.

"Good morning," said Jonathan. He introduced Vasil to them, and everyone sat down. A robot brought cakes, fruit, and lemonade.

"What do you think of your new Center?" Gretchen asked.

"Well—" Perkin looked tense and uncomfortable.

"It's so much brighter and airier than the old one," Judy said with a nervous smile.

"I insisted on that," Jonathan said. "The dark halls used to bother me, but I loved the patios and all the sunshine. Have you got all the supplies and people you need?"

"Yes, thank you," Perkin said. "It's more than I ever imagined. The old Center was nothing compared to this. The equipment, the resources, the people—I'd thought it would be awkward working with non-Intertel people, but it's working out very well."

"Well, we wanted you to have the best people in the world, not just corp members," Gretchen said.

"Maybe that's why we're doing a hundred implants a day," said Phil Haddad. "After all the fuss we made over you guys, now it's like having your tonsils out." Vasil looked suspiciously at him.

"We'll be up to five hundred a day by the end of the summer," Judy added. "And other centers will be operating by then as well. You'll have your half million implants by the end of next year."

"What will you do then?" asked Phil.

Jonathan shrugged. "The more people who join the net, the more ideas we have. A lot of us want to build starships."

"A lot of us," Perkin echoed. "You still have individuality, even when you share so many minds?"

"Too right," Gretchen said. "Sometimes we fight like mad, and we can still close ourselves off if we want a little peace and quiet. This starship business, now— Jonathan's against it, the silly bugger, but I think it's a great idea."

Jonathan looked long-suffering. "It'll be a waste of effort, Gretch. The extrapolations are perfectly clear that within five years—well, ten, anyway—we'll be able to use topological resonance to go anywhere we like across a couple of thousand light-years, instantly. Your starships wouldn't even be out of the Oort Cloud by then."

"Wishful thinking!"

"Wishful thinking is what got us all here."

Vasil nudged Jonathan. "Come on," he muttered.

"I'm sorry, Vaz. We'd like you to do us a favor, Dr. Perkin. Vasil wants an implant."

"But he's not . . . defective."

"I know. Even so, we want him in the net."

For some time Perkin said nothing. Judy glanced worriedly at him. At last he spoke. "I suppose this is some kind of ironic retribution, isn't it? After all these years of supposedly mistreating nonstats, now we're being treated the same way."

Jonathan looked surprised. "What do you mean?"

"You take over the world, you overthrow the social system, and you start pulling every defective you can find into this 'net' of yours. Obviously it's all working beautifully for you. Your enterprises have already started making more money than the Consortium ever dreamed of. In just a few weeks you've doubled the total of human knowledge, and you've invented machines and processes no one ever imagined. Six months ago you were in diapers, and now you're God's own executive assistants. Now you're bringing in underclass thugs and we just have to do as we're told. We're just your servants."

"You used to be Claudio Chang's servants," said Jonathan. "And that was for life. You'll work for us for just a little while longer."

"What does that mean? Are you going to toss us aside when you don't need us anymore?"

"Well, that's what you did with the patrons," said Jonathan. "They weren't needed to work, just to consume, so you let them fiddle their lives away with egographies and war games and soapers."

"And that's good enough for us as well," said Perkin bitterly. "Never mind our skills, or what we've done for you."

"Duane, please," Judy begged. He ignored her.

"You were going to cut us open to see how our implants were working," Gretchen reminded him.

"I almost wish I had," Perkin said harshly. "You've
been using us all along. The turings gave me the idea for
the implant. They made sure I got what I needed, and all
the time I thought I was in charge. Now you've given me
this shiny new laboratory, but I'm still the jerk who
does the implants."

"For a while you'll do the implants. Then you'll get
one yourself," Jonathan said.

Perkin stared at him. "As a reward?"

"No. But after we have all the defectives in the net,
we'll bring in all the patrons who want to join, and then
the old upstatus people."

"Why? Why bother?"

Jonathan looked surprised at the question. "With
every person we add to the net, it gets stronger and
better. We don't want to leave anybody out."

Perkin smiled unpleasantly. "Brain surgery for three
billion people, just to suck them into your anthill?"

"Oh, no. We're already working on an implant that'll
stick to the skin. Eventually we'll build a genetic con-
stellation so people can be born receptive to the net."

"Impossible."

"No. We're just starting to learn what we can do."

Perkin steepled his fingers, very much like Captain
Nemo, and looked coldly at Jonathan. "I suppose you
are. But I have my own values, my own individual integrity. I don't choose to be . . . submerged in a sea of
other minds. I'll work for you, but I won't join you."

"As you choose," Jonathan said.

"D'you ever see an old Japanese painting?" Gretchen
asked suddenly. "You see a boat down low in the water,
trying to get to shore. Mount Fuji is off in the distance.
But right over the boat is a huge wave looking bloody
awful, just about to fall. Well, that was the way we used
to be, sitting in our crippled bodies, waiting to be destroyed. But now we're the wave, and we're Mount Fuji
too. I'm looking at you, and at the same time I'm looking down on the whole world from the satellites and

spacehabs, and looking out at the whole universe. Nothing in the world can really hurt us anymore. We *are* the world, and we'll last as long as it does.''

Perkin looked out across the balcony to the gleaming houses of Rand Mountain, that once had seemed so far away and now seemed so close. He caught Judy's eye and was comforted by her smile.

''Well,'' he said briskly. ''We'd better get Vasil ready. You're sure you want this, now?''

''Pure sure. Sir.''

''All right. Come on; I'll show you to your room. No, don't get up,'' he added to Jonathan and Gretchen. ''I'll be back in a few minutes.''

Jonathan and Gretchen embraced Vasil, who looked nervous but eager as he turned to accompany Perkin. They walked into one of the sunlit corridors; Perkin talked easily and fluently about the procedure, but his thoughts turned restlessly on one question: How had Gretchen known about the picture of the wave and the boat?

He suspected he could find out only one way—by leaving the boat and becoming part of the wave that soon would fill the world with its endless joyous roar.

MORE SCIENCE FICTION ADVENTURE!

BESTSELLING
Science Fiction
and
Fantasy

☐ 47810-7	**THE LEFT HAND OF DARKNESS,** Ursula K. Le Guin	$2.95
☐ 16021-2	**DORSAI!,** Gordon R. Dickson	$2.95
☐ 80583-3	**THIEVES' WORLD,**™ Robert Lynn Asprin, editor	$2.95
☐ 11456-3	**CONAN #1,** Robert E. Howard, L. Sprague de Camp, Lin Carter	$2.75
☐ 49142-1	**LORD DARCY INVESTIGATES,** Randall Garrett	$2.75
☐ 21889-X	**EXPANDED UNIVERSE,** Robert A. Heinlein	$3.95
☐ 87330-8	**THE WARLOCK UNLOCKED,** Christopher Stasheff	$2.95
☐ 05480-3	**BERSERKER,** Fred Saberhagen	$2.75
☐ 10264-6	**CHANGELING,** Roger Zelazny	$2.95
☐ 51553-3	**THE MAGIC GOES AWAY,** Larry Niven	$2.95

Prices may be slightly higher in Canada.

Available at your local bookstore or return this form to:

ACE SCIENCE FICTION
Book Mailing Service
P.O. Box 690, Rockville Centre, NY 11571

Please send me the titles checked above. I enclose _____ Include 75¢ for postage and handling if one book is ordered; 25¢ per book for two or more not to exceed $1.75. California, Illinois, New York and Tennessee residents please add sales tax.

NAME_____

ADDRESS_____

CITY_____STATE/ZIP_____

(allow six weeks for delivery)   SF 9